LOVE IN THE CRETACEOUS

HOWARD W. ROBERTSON

ANAPHORA LITERARY PRESS

BROWNSVILLE, TEXAS

ANAPHORA LITERARY PRESS
1898 Athens Street
Brownsville, TX 78520
https://anaphoraliterary.com

Book design by Anna Faktorovich, Ph.D.

Printed in the United States of America, United Kingdom and in Australia on acid-free paper.

Published in 2017 by Anaphora Literary Press

Love in the Cretaceous
Howard W. Robertson—1st edition.

Library of Congress Control Number: 2017905568

Library Cataloging Information
Robertson, Howard W., 1947-, author.
    Love in the Cretaceous / Howard W. Robertson
    130 p. ; 9 in.
    ISBN 978-1-68114-332-3 (softcover : alk. paper)
    ISBN 978-1-68114-333-0 (hardcover : alk. paper)
    ISBN 978-1-68114-334-7 (e-book)
1. Fiction—Science Fiction—Apocalyptic & Post-Apocalyptic.
2. Nature—Dinosaurs & Prehistoric Creatures.
3. Fiction—Science Fiction—Genetic Engineering. I. Title.
PN3427-3448: Prose Fiction: Special kinds of fiction: Fiction genres
813: American fiction in English

LOVE IN THE CRETACEOUS

HOWARD W. ROBERTSON

CONTENTS

SKOOKUM

The roar of a T-rex is like a hundred lions in your ear.

Bud shouts, "Merry Christmas to you too, Dorothy."

That's what we call her. We give all the dinosaurs pet names.

Lana gives a polite chuckle and continues her work. She drives the forklift up to the small pile of dead sheep and loads one onto the fork.

Bud has trucked the carcasses out here to the T-rex pen and dumped them. I say "pen," but it's a five-mile by three-mile area with Skookum Creek running through the middle of it. The catapult is a bit uphill, so we can see over the high, massive wall made of reinforced concrete.

Lana sets the sheep onto the catapult and gets down from the forklift.

Dorothy is waiting and watching from the other side of the wall. She has heard us coming in the truck and knows we're going to feed her.

Bud says, "Dorothy knows the drill."

He always says that.

Lana launches the sheep's body, and it flies heavily over the wall, landing with a thud on the other side.

Dorothy roars again, even louder than before. The hackles rise on my neck, and a small electric charge surges up my spine, causing me to shiver briefly.

Dorothy is forty feet long and weighs twelve thousand pounds. She has feet like a giant bird because birds are her close relatives. Archaeopteryx, the first bird, was a small theropod in the late Jurassic; T-rex is a giant theropod that didn't come along until the Late Cretaceous more than eighty million years later. The Steller's jays and ravens that flit through the towering conifers around Dorothy are dinosaurs too, members of her extended family really.

Paleontologists know from fossils that the thigh bones of T-rex were warmer at the core than at the surface and that the degree of temperature difference was much greater than today's cold-blooded reptiles but significantly less than modern warm-blooded mammals. So T-rex was somewhat warm-blooded, hemiendothermic. That's why we're out here around noon when, thanks to climate change, it's over eighty degrees on December 24, 2116. We had the geneticists put this hemiendothermism into the genome when we were designing our re-creation of T-rex, so Dorothy is much more vigorous now in the middle of the day than she was in the early morning.

Lana loads up another sheep and catapults it into the pen.

At this point, Dorothy does something out of the ordinary. She roars again, but this time it's different, much less menacing, musical really. It's a cry of love. She's calling to Roger, the male T-rex who shares the pen with her. She's basically offering him some of the food, buying him dinner, as it were. She can do this because we had her designed to be bigger than the male, since T-rex was a dimorphic species.

Usually, Bud and Lana would drive around to the other end of the pen five miles away and feed Roger there while Dorothy was safely occupied with her own ration of dead sheep. They won't need to do that today. Sure enough, Roger understands her intent and comes running. Well, loping is more like it. Paleontologists can tell from the strength of the thigh bone fossils that T-rex couldn't gallop, so we've had our two specimens designed to run at about seven miles an hour.

Roger slows down as he nears Dorothy. He stops and pushes his nostrils forward and up, obviously trying to sniff out the meaningful scent of the situation. We know from fossil skulls what shape the brain was. We can tell that the olfactory area of the brain was very large, indicating a keen sense of smell. We put that into the genome too. Dorothy must be giving off the scent of a sexually receptive female, because Roger moves forward, approaches the food, and eagerly eats, knowing she will allow it this time. Lana keeps lobbing in sheep all the while. When Roger has had his fill, he adroitly moves to Dorothy's rear and vigorously copulates with her.

It's exciting to watch.

I look over at Bud. He's a sturdy man of medium height, fifty years old, with greying black hair. He has an artificial right arm. He lost his limb working with farm equipment here at Cretaceous World more than a decade ago.

Bud winks at me and says, "Atta boy, Roger!"

I peek at Lana out of the corner of my eye. She's a thin, athletic woman of around thirty with a long blonde ponytail. She grew up on a ranch in Eastern Oregon near Pendleton, and she's a tough cookie. Her blue eyes look a little glassy with arousal now, but she stands perfectly still and just watches.

Dorothy will lay eggs, but they won't hatch. We can't handle a population increase in our dinosaurs. When one of them dies, we just make a new one. Our genetic engineers are real wizards. A T-rex would only live thirty years at most in the Cretaceous Period when its life was very violent. The fossil record shows many broken bones for T-rex, especially broken legs from falling down. Living this easy life here with us, Dorothy and Roger are expected to live much longer.

I leave Bud and Lana there to continue their work catapulting food into the T-rex pen. As I drive back to headquarters, I stop by the side of the private road where Skookum Creek runs right next to it. I look at the creek and recollect the meanings of the word "skookum" in the Chinook Jargon: strong, brave, a demon, a ghost, a spirit.

From a couple miles away now, I hear Dorothy roar again and then Roger. Skookum, yes, skookum indeed.

* * * * * * * * * * * *

Becky's luminous green eyes enchant people. They enchant me. I'm standing in five-foot water, holding her in my arms, gazing languidly into the liquid pools of her enchanting green eyes.

After I left Bud and Lana, I returned to the residence.

That's what we call it, "the residence." It refers to the palatial edifice that Becky and I are privileged to inhabit as the reigning executives who guide the complex corporate entity known as Cretaceous World.

I took the long way home to the residence, since I was just basically checking on our daily operations, keeping in touch with what was going on at our vast amusement park full of genetically engineered dinosaurs.

I drove past the subway station near the main gate where visitors were busy boarding the one o'clock train in order to travel to observation stations around the park. This was the very best time to go take a look at the dinosaurs because this was when they're most active and out and about at spots where they're observable. There were quite a few people visiting the park today, even though Christmas Eve was just a few hours away. The parking structure near the main gate looked pretty full, and I could see through the windows of the large restaurant and the sizeable gift shop that plenty of folks were in both these places. I continued on past the museum full of dinosaur fossils from all over the world, and there were plenty of people going in there as well. I next came to the sprawling apartment building where the park's hundreds of employees lived.

We call this building "the bunkhouse."

Further uphill was the office building where the bureaucracy was located, the middle managers and office assistants who administered the park.

We call this place "the headquarters."

Alongside it was the physical plant, the place where the physical operation of the park was coordinated: electrical matters, plumbing, heating, cooling, road repair, park security, and so forth.

We just call this "the plant."

I arrived finally at the residence, the palace that sat highest, majestically overlooking all.

The residence is where I live now, a humble retired professor of microbiology who has been picked by his old classmate from undergrad days at USC to be the CEO guiding this whole affair, plucked from obscurity by his old college chum who has gone on to amass a colossal fortune in various software enterprises and who has built and continued to fund this amazing place, this noble attempt to connect global humanity viscerally with the history of life on Earth, this brilliant spot in the Coast Range of Western Oregon, this imagination-igniting theme park called Cretaceous World.

The valet met me in the circular driveway and took the car behind the palace to the capacious carriage house for our many vehicles. As I progressed along the wide walkway to the massive double doors of the front entrance, I regarded the gleaming white magnificence of the three wide-spreading stories of this grand edifice with the narrow cylindrical fourth floor crowning it all.

We call this lofty cylinder on top "the tower."

Chandler greeted me at the front doors, "Welcome home, sir."

I said, "Good to be home, Chandler. How goes it this fine afternoon?"

The corners of his mouth turned slightly upward, and he replied, "Very well, sir. Thank you."

I inquired, "Where might I find the lady of the house?"

His eyes twinkled, and he informed me, "Madam is in the gym, sir. Specifically in the pool, I believe."

I thanked him and climbed the spiral staircase in the middle of the cavernous entry hall. I went to the master bedroom on the third floor and changed into swimming trunks. Then I strolled down the hall to the gym and went in. I walked past the superb array of aerobic machines and weight machines, past the whirlpool bath and the sauna, to the Olympic-sized swimming pool where I found my charming wife.

She shouted, "Hey!"

I answered, "Hey!"

That's how we typically greet each other. After 35 years of marriage, we keep it simple. It works well for us.

I asked, "What'd you do this morning?"

She said, "I went down to the headquarters and the plant, walked around a little, mostly talked with office assistants. On the way home, I swung by the bunkhouse and strolled around there a bit."

I said, "I was with Bud and Lana feeding the T-rexes."

She suggested, "Why don't you hop in? The water's fine."

I didn't just hop in: I did a cannonball. Then I swam over to her and embraced her.

She wraps her legs around me, and here I am, standing in five-foot water, holding her in my arms, gazing into the liquid pools of her enchanting green eyes.

I say, "I felt like a Spinosaur coming across the pool."

She smiles and says, "If you were a Spinosaur, you'd probably take me out to deeper water."

I agree, "Probably."

I like the feeling of her arms around my neck.

I say, "I saw something at the T-rex pen today."

She says, "Oh yeah, like what?"

I explain, "Dorothy invited Roger to have sex with her, and he did."

Her eyes widen, and she comments, "Wow, sounds stimulating."

The technology of erectile pills has come a long way. Thanks to this progress, a 68-year-old man like me now has as strong an erection as Roger's.

I hold Becky up with one arm and pull my trunks down with the other hand so they slide off my legs. I move the divider on her bikini bottom aside a little and enter her. I roar like Roger. She laughs and roars back.

* * * * * * * * * * * *

I'm suddenly awake. I look over at the clock and see it's a little after midnight. I get up quietly so as not to wake my sleeping wife and climb the spiral stairs to the tower, which is directly over the master bedroom.

The tower is a circular room with a large radius. There are floor to ceiling windows all the way around it. I stand looking south over Cretaceous World. It's raining outside. I see the lights of the headquarters and the plant, of the bunkhouse further down, and of the museum, the restaurant, the gift shop, the parking garage, and the subway station down by the entry portal. I see a security car patrolling slowly. Otherwise, all is darkness.

It's very early on Christmas Day now. I imagine I'm a little kid who can't sleep waiting for Santa Claus. I go to the shelves of the book stacks at the north end of the tower. I find the Greek New Testament and take it to the recliner sofa at the center of the room's circle. As I always do on this day, I turn to the Nativity section of the Gospel of Luke and read of the amazing births of John the Baptist and Jesus Christ.

1:13-14 - εἶπεν δὲ πρὸς αὐτὸν ὁ ἄγγελος, Μὴ φοβοῦ, Ζαχαρία, διότι εἰσηκούσθη ἡ δέησίς σου, καὶ ἡ γυνή σου Ἐλισάβετ γεννήσει υἱόν σοι, καὶ καλέσεις τὸ ὄνομα αὐτοῦ Ἰωάννην. καὶ ἔσται χαρά σοι καὶ ἀγαλλίασις.

"And the angel said to him, 'Don't be afraid, Zacharias, because your entreaty has been heard and your wife Elizabeth will bear your son; and you will call his name John, and joy and exultation will be yours.'"

Elizabeth was well along in years and barren. Zacharias and she had no child. Then the angel came with the message.

1:39-41 - Ἀναστᾶσα δὲ Μαριὰμ ἐν ταῖς ἡμέραις ταύταις ἐπορεύθη εἰς τὴν ὀρεινὴν μετὰ σπουδῆς εἰς πόλιν Ἰούδα, καὶ εἰσῆλθεν εἰς τὸν οἶκον Ζαχαρίου καὶ ἠσπάσατο τὴν Ἐλισάβετ. καὶ ἐγένετο ὡς ἤκουσεν τὸν ἀσπασμὸν τῆς Μαρίας ἡ Ἐλισάβετ, ἐσκίρτησεν τὸ βρέφος ἐν τῇ κοιλίᾳ αὐτῆς, καὶ ἐπλήσθη πνεύματος ἁγίου ἡ Ἐλισάβετ.

"And Mary, having risen, went with haste in these days into the mountainous country to a city of Judah and entered the house of Zacharias and greeted Elizabeth. And it happened that, as Elizabeth heard the greeting of Mary, the infant leaped in her womb, and Elizabeth was filled with the holy spirit."

Tonight, I'm focused on Elizabeth, this old childless woman who was able miraculously to give birth to a son who grew up to make a difference in the world.

Becky and I never had a child. We're old now. We never thought we wanted kids. We had our careers. We met in the Biology Department of the State University of New Geneva less than a hundred miles east of here over in the Upper Willamette Valley. She was a professor of botany who'd come to SUNG from graduate school at the Ohio State University. From USC, I'd gone on to graduate school at UC Berkeley, where I'd become a microbiologist fascinated by the four billion years of cellular life on Earth. Becky and I'd just wanted to read, to think, to write, to teach. Children had no appeal at all. Now at age 68 on this dark and rainy night, I can't help wondering and wishing.

When I was a kid in Woodland Hills in the San Fernando Valley, I knew a woman who was a mother of two young children. I knew her very well. She seduced me, and I had sex with her for a summer. She was thirty-eight, I was eighteen, and her daughter and son were eleven and eight respectively. Her husband was an executive in the recording industry. He'd become impotent from something the pills couldn't fix, something that came from losing interest in sex, in life, with her anyway. She was a counselor at my high school, and as soon as I graduated, there she was, calling me on the phone, inviting me over when her husband was away. She became convinced that she could divorce her aging husband and marry me. She thought that would work. We'd be one big happy family living off the alimony and child support. At the time, I was tempted. Now I know how many ways that could've, would've gone wrong. I went off to USC where I lived in a dorm on-campus, and she faded away. Driving down to South Central Los Angeles from the west end of the Valley was too hard a reality to overcome, and her living nearby was out of the question. She had an aversion to poverty and gunfire. It could have been a real mess if I'd made her pregnant. As it was, it was just over. I would've impregnated her if she'd wanted me to. She wouldn't have had to trick me or anything. I wanted to fill her with my seed. I'd had no idea what I would've been getting into. My biology was all in favor of the project; my becoming a biologist would likely have been a casualty of it. That was a close call. And yet, if I'd plunged into all that, I'd have a child now, probably children.

I think of Dorothy, of how her eggs will never hatch because it would be most inconvenient for us. I wonder if she cares at all about that.

I finish reading about the wondrous birth of the Christ-child and return down the spiral stairs to my sleeping wife and my king-size bed. I crawl in and pull the covers up around my face. I think of Roger. I think of being in the pool and roaring like Roger. I think of Becky roaring back. God, I love her.

TARZANA

Harold well remembers the day his destiny changed. Not a night goes by that he doesn't think about it.

He was driving east on the Ventura Freeway, heading from his cozy apartment in Tarzana to his current acting gig at a TV studio in Burbank. It was a minor part. That's the only kind he ever got. He was resigned by then to calling himself a character actor. It could've been worse. At least he could find work. Most of the aspiring actors in LA earned their meager living as waiters in restaurants and cafes. This had been so for a century and a half. Harold never had to wait long for the next part to come along. He always had lines to say, and the lines were usually important enough to make it into the final cut. Millions of people recognized his face when they saw it on the screen. Very few could remember what his name was.

He was driving along admiring the majestic San Gabriel Mountains, which were clearly visible to the east now that all vehicles were electric and thick smog was a thing of the past. Without warning, the Earth lurched beneath his wheels and kept on lurching. As it did for most everyone in LA at that moment, the word "EARTHQUAKE" flashed in his mind and kept on flashing.

The expectation of all those who'd lived there for a long time was that it would probably stop after thirty seconds or less. It didn't. It kept on shaking hard for nearly five minutes. The first minute seemed like an hour, the second minute seemed like a day, the third like a week, the fourth like the end of the world, and the fifth just seemed utterly beyond belief. This was the Big One, the long-awaited giant earthquake that registered 8.0 or more on the Richter scale. Actually 8.3, it was later announced.

Harold and most of his fellow drivers reflexively slowed down, way down, coming to a full stop before very long. Others didn't, and they each rammed into the vehicle in front, so that loud crashes burst forth all along the freeway.

The road-surface shifted and cracked everywhere. Overpasses and cloverleaf interchanges crumbled onto the cars stopped beneath them. People began bleeding and dying. Fires from rear-ended vehicles sent plumes of smoke up from one end of the San Fernando Valley to the other. Gasoline was no longer present in vehicles or the carnage would've been much worse.

The transitional era of natural gas was also long over, so natural gas pipes going to buildings weren't a factor. Massive explosions would've been everywhere if there'd still been gas in all those cracked pipes.

Water pipes broke all over the place, and the city's entire water supply rapidly drained out into the desert soil.

Emergency vehicles couldn't get through to help the wounded. Many died from injuries that wouldn't normally have been considered life-threatening.

Some people took advantage of the disorder to mug their fellow earthquake victims. Police couldn't do anything about it.

Brush fires alongside the roads through the canyons spread and became raging wildfires that ran away like wild horses across the hills. Fire trucks just couldn't get to them.

Sewage pipes ruptured everywhere, as would become malodorously evident in the days that followed. The entire city smelled like aging garbage.

And all this was just the beginning of the nightmare that got much worse before it began to get better and that lasted for seemingly interminable months.

When Harold could get out of LA, he did. He'd heard nice things about Oregon, so he went there. His agent, who'd relocated to Seattle, told him about an unusual acting job at Cretaceous World, the dinosaur park that was just about to open. He went for an interview.

He got the part. He was by far the most qualified candidate who applied for the job, which was to play the role of Chandler, the butler at the palatial mansion where the managers of the park lived. He would have three understudy actors under his direction. They'd be available to substitute in the role any time he liked. This would give him great flexibility with his time. The understudy actors would be cast to look and sound like the lead actor, which would be Harold, now that he was hired. He'd participate in picking the understudy actors, including fully taking part in the interview process. The goal was to simulate a single nineteenth-century English butler but to do it without the morally offensive class system. Harold saw it as a kind of ongoing performance piece which he'd both be acting in and directing. He and his understudies would collectively do the actual work of one full-time Victorian butler. The pay was nearly twice what he'd been making in Los Angeles, he'd have generous health and retirement benefits, and he'd live rent-free in sumptuous quarters at the mansion.

His agent asked, "What's not to like?"

He agreed, "Not a thing. Of course, I'll have to give up my dream of winning an Oscar or an Emmy."

He laughed. So did his agent. He thought maybe she laughed a little too hard, but he didn't make a big deal out of it.

* * * * * * * * * * * *

Ronnie asks, "You sure I can't persuade you to come with me to the Bijou tonight?"

Harold says, "No, I'll be there tomorrow. Friday will be better. Bigger crowd."

Harold and Ronnie are married. Ronnie is a svelte young man with bleached blond hair. Harold is much older.

They live in a 3,000-square foot suite in the manorial residence where Harold is the lead actor in the role of Chandler the butler. His employment earns him the right to live in this suite with his family, however defined. One thing about Cretaceous World: when they decide they want to keep you, they give you such a good situation that you won't be tempted to go elsewhere.

Ronnie runs the Bijou Theater in the neighboring town of Dewberry. The theater shows classic movies, art films, and new or recent movies of especially high quality. It would be possible to watch at home everything they show at the Bijou. What the theater does is provide a big screen and a communal experience. There's a café in the lobby where people gather before and after the show.

This week in February 2117 is a Harold Robinson festival at the Bijou. Movies and television episodes in which Ronnie's spouse played a significant role will be shown at a rate of two or three a night. The great man himself, a big fish in a small pond, will make his appearance on Friday and Saturday nights, sign autographs, and rub elbows with the crowd of admirers. It's big fun for one and all.

Harold says, "You know you've changed since I first knew you."

Ronnie asks, "How so, dear?"

Harold replies, "You were content then to stand back and watch the drama that life presented. Now you want to take action and play a part in the movie."

Ronnie says, "It's true. All the world's a movie: I still want to sit in the audience and watch, sure, but I also want to be up on the screen. I want to play a role, even if a small one."

Harold smiles, "My boy has grown up. Daddy's proud."

Ronnie says, "Say, pops, maybe you can lend me a bit of your wisdom."

Harold keeps smiling, "You want a few wise words from the graybeard?"

Ronnie nods yes.

Harold asks, "How may I be of service, young man?"

Ronnie says, "You know the reading series I just started at the theater?"

Harold says, "The Dewberry Community Writers Series. Love that name."

Ronnie explains, "Yes, well, I've got a problem with the next reading in the series, and I'm not sure what to do."

Harold watches and waits.

Ronnie continues, "My idea has been to make a video of each reader and put it up on the Internet so that what we do here can be seen by the whole wide world for years to come."

Harold asks rhetorically, "Where are the readings of yesteryear? Ubi sunt?"

Ronnie brightens, "Exactly. So now all of a sudden just two weeks before the reading, Elizabeth Martin doesn't want a recording of her performance to be made."

Harold asks, "Why not?"

Ronnie becomes agitated, "She won't say why! She acts like I'm making her a well-intentioned offer, which she appreciates, but no thanks, she'd rather not. She lies and pretends she didn't understand that being recorded was a clearly stated part of the agreement to perform. She gives no reason at all for why she now objects. When I press her for an explanation, her tone becomes angry. She's outraged that I don't just accept and honor her wishes with a generous good grace."

Harold inquires, "Why don't you?"

Ronnie's tone becomes sharp and shrill, "Why should I? I'm doing the work. I have a right to do my reading series any way I like. Who does she think she is, Queen Elizabeth the First?"

Harold doesn't smile, though he feels like it.

Ronnie grins sheepishly, "Thank you."

Harold asks, "For what?"

Ronnie says, "You know what: for not smiling."

Harold smiles, "You're welcome."

Ronnie says again, "I don't know what to do. I know it's a trivial matter. I know I shouldn't let it get to me. I know I should be the bigger person."

Harold continues with his wise smile, "Actors are always either prima donnas or cool cats. A person reading a literary work to an audience is a kind of actor. You've got a minor problem with a prima donna. This should be a simple matter to resolve. You're sure it's too late to change readers?"

Ronnie says mournfully, "The publicity has already gone out. Plus lots of people admire Elizabeth. She has a lot of friends. I don't want to be hated by them all. I don't want to be the ogre that's abusing the princess."

Harold asks, "And you want me to show you the way out of the stubborn though petty dilemma in which you find yourself mired?"

Ronnie nods, "If you wouldn't mind, dear."

Harold says, "Very well. If you don't insist on doing the series in the way that brings you joy, you'll stop loving it. The desire to do it will die inside you. You'll also be ashamed of yourself for not defending your dream."

Ronnie is listening intently.

Harold continues, "So you have no choice really. You must drop proud Queen Elizabeth and replace her with a writer who doesn't object to being recorded and shown around the planet for time to come. You can tell her that if she withdraws her objection immediately and agrees to be videorecorded, if she does this with good will and without any resentment, then her reading can proceed as planned. You should add that you'll assume she won't and in fact can't do that. You should tell her that you'll replace her unless you receive her abject capitulation in the next twenty-four hours. Don't put it in those terms, of course, but be clear that's what you mean."

Ronnie is staring at him with eyes wide.

Harold concludes, "If you like, I'll agree to be her replacement as a reader. You can announce it every night during the festival that I'll be reading from my memoirs at the next reading in your series. Send Queen Elizabeth a message now before you leave so that you can begin your publicity for me tomorrow night during my appearance at the festival. The word will get around at the speed of lightning. Just tell people you hope to include Liz in a later reading. It could happen, you know. She may wise up and get with your program. Meanwhile, your next reading will be a glorious success. People love me around these parts. They'll be glad you've coaxed me out into a public performance."

Ronnie's mouth is hanging open, and he reaches up under his chin and pushes it shut. He's joking, but he means it too. He's impressed and amazed by his spouse.

Harold shrugs, "I learned a few things while I was in Hollywood."

* * * * * * * * * * * *

Harold is sitting on the couch in the living room of his suite. Ronnie has just left for the Bijou. Harold is lost in the memory of having arrived here so long ago from the devastation of Tarzana in order to interview for the part of Chandler the butler.

Becky herself answered the big front doors when he rang the bell back then. She was wearing casual clothes and her hair was woven in a thick braid that hung down her back. He was impressed with her enchanting green eyes.

She led him on a leisurely stroll around the cavernous sprawl of the impressive building. She showed him the luxurious quarters that would be his if he was offered the part and accepted it.

After the tour, they sat together in the tea room on the second floor.

Becky said, "If Chandler were on duty, he would bring us tea now."

Harold enjoyed the gentle humor.

Becky inquired, "So you were in LA when the Big One hit. That must have been terrifying."

Harold said, "Yes, you could say that. It left me with the strong desire to be somewhere else."

She said, "Understandable."

He said, "I don't want to seem fearful, but what earthquake planning has gone into the design and construction of Cretaceous World? I understand that the Cascadia subduction zone up here could cause an even stronger quake than the one I lived through along the San

Andreas Fault."

She observed, "You've done your homework."

He shrugged and waited.

She said, "As you must know, the Cascadia subduction zone runs from Cape Mendocino to Vancouver Island, 620 miles long. It lies offshore in the Pacific Ocean about a hundred miles from where we're now sitting. The distance helps us, of course, but the quakes it produces are just so big that the danger is still extreme. The last earthquake it caused was an estimated 9.2 on the Richter scale. That one was around 1700. We think they come along every 400-600 years. We don't really know that though. The next big Cascadia quake could happen before you and I are done talking today."

He felt a thrill of fear rush up his spine upon hearing those words.

She continued, "Our location here in the mountains of the Coast Range gives us the elevation and shielding we need from the giant tsunami that will devastate the coastal areas. All our buildings and other structures here were built to withstand even the most powerful earthquake. The direct damage to them would be minor. What we can't do much about, however, is the liquefaction of the soil. The shaking will turn it into a thick brown liquid that will pour down every available slope. Once the shaking stops, it will turn back into solid ground. The thick walls of the dinosaur pens won't rupture, but the liquefaction will fill in around them. The dinosaurs will be able to walk right over the walls and out of the enclosures."

Harold gasped, "The dinosaurs will escape?"

Becky sighed, "Yes, there's no way we can prevent that, assuming that the liquefacted soil hasn't already trapped them, poured in around their legs and bodies and then hardened. Either way, we'll have to kill them and have our genetic engineers make replacements. We've developed a complete response plan with the Oregon National Guard. Missile-firing helicopters and drones will track the dinosaurs down and blow them up. There are only nine pairs of dinosaurs here, so it won't be that hard to do it quickly. All airport runways and paved roads will be cracked and buckled, naturally, which rules out fighter planes or tanks as an option."

He said, "I remember the cracked roads of Tarzana. That's where I lived. I was just leaving for work on the Ventura Freeway. I'll never get that image out of my head."

Ted appeared in the tea room at this point. These were the Beebes, the managers of Cretaceous World, the rulers of the realm. This grand manor was theirs. If Harold landed this gig, he'd be playing their servant for the foreseeable future.

Ted asked, "Can I interest you in a tour of the park?"

Harold noticed the natural gravitas of this tall gentleman.

Harold looked at Becky before answering.

Becky said, "We thought it would be good for you to see the park before we get into the details of the interview."

Harold slipped into the persona of Chandler, "As you wish, madam."

He bowed his head toward Ted and said, "Sir."

TUMTUM

It takes your breath away to see a Brontosaur run.

Bud sees the two of them thundering towards us though and has plenty of breath left to holler, "And down the stretch they come!"

We know from fossil thigh-bones that Brontosaurs were capable of a slow run, so we designed our pair to do about a dozen miles per hour. To see an animal 70 feet long and weighing 50,000 pounds move that fast seems nothing less than miraculous.

Lana has used the giant crane to drop a couple tons of mixed ferns, horsetails, and gingko and araucarian leaves into the Brontosaur area. The crane is 50 feet high with a long arm so the two sauropods won't bang their heads on it, since they can only reach up to about 25 feet with their long necks.

It's May 2117, and the angiosperms are in bloom all around these two colossal creatures from the end of the Jurassic. We called it close enough and just sort of rolled them into Cretaceous World, our magnificent dinosaur park. Brontosaurs flourished around 150 million years ago, well before the rise of the flowering plants about 30 million years later in the Cretaceous period. When our genetic engineers designed the genome for our pair, they tried to make them as authentic as possible, so the two of them really prefer the kind of food they would have eaten way back when. That's why they come running at feeding time when we give them the ancient gymnosperms that they like best. There's actually a large nursery in the neighboring town of Dewberry that's dedicated to supplying our herbivores with food from the time of the dinosaurs.

Lana gets down out of the crane and walks over to me.

She says, "I'd sure like to see a whole herd of these moving together."

Lana has a Ph.D. in paleontology from SUNG and knows full well why we couldn't handle that. Our pen of seven miles by four miles is barely big enough for the two Brontosaurs we do have. By the way, I'm so glad the alternate name has died away over the past hundred years: "thunder lizard" is so much more appropriate for these giants than "deceptive lizard."

I say, "Wouldn't that be grand?"

She smiles and tosses her long blonde ponytail. Then she goes over to Bud and gives him an assignment to do.

Lana is actually Bud's supervisor, though her youthfulness and the flecks of grey everywhere in Bud's hair might suggest the opposite. Bud drove a big rig longhaul for over a decade before joining our staff here at Cretaceous World. He's happy as a clam here. We offer generous salary, great job security, comprehensive health benefits, a month's paid vacation, and a rock-solid pension. Not bad for a high school graduate from Roseburg.

Lana returns to my side and says, "Really, I love imagining the whole herds of these guys that roamed around Western Laurasia."

I enjoy it that she knows it's Laurasia still and not yet Laramidia, since the Brontosaur was in the late Jurassic, 50 million years before Laramidia formed.

She says, "Have you ever heard them crack their tails like bull-whips? It's amazing. You can imagine that they could knock over an Allosaur with their tails and then just stomp on it with their huge clawed feet. Once they got big like this, they really didn't have much to fear from predators."

I say, "I understand they grew very fast when they were young, and then once they were full-grown, they could live well past a hundred years."

She says, "Yeah, some paleontologists speculate about three hundred years as a reasonable guess for how long a Brontosaur could live."

I say, "I spent the early part of my career studying the smallest of single-celled life-forms who could basically live forever if conditions were right. Bacteria had no programmed cell-death. It wasn't until the larger nucleated cells came along that death from old age became possible."

She says, "You started out with the tiniest living beings who began around four billion years ago. Bruce and Phyllis here must seem like giant newcomers to you."

I enjoy her use of the nicknames the crew gave the Brontosaur couple.

I say, "The Cambrian explosion changed everything. Between 600 and 500 million years ago, life got larger fast. In a few blinks of geologic time, the sauropods were leaving their footprints all over the landscape of the Morrison Formation not so far from here."

She says, "You've covered all of life on Earth in your career, from tiny beginning to the recent hugeness. Nice."

We pause and watch Bruce and Phyllis enjoy their meal.

She asks, "Do you think we mammals would've taken over from the dinosaurs if the big asteroid hadn't hit the Gulf of Mexico?"

I reply, "I doubt it. We were just scurrying around the margins and doing things at night when our fully warm-blooded metabolism gave us an advantage. The dinosaurs were the most successful animals ever to stride the Earth and would've continued to dominate us. Their demise was our golden opportunity."

She smiles and goes off with Bud, who has finished his task and returned.

* * * * * * * * * * *

After watching the feeding of the Brontosaurs, I return to the residence. It always makes me childishly happy to come home to the palace that Becky and I are privileged to inhabit. I don't like to think of myself as a superficial person, but in this one regard, I'm really quite shallow.

Chandler greets me at the entrance in his usual cheery way.

I say, "I'm going up to the tea room. Please bring me a bowl of fresh strawberries and a big pot of tea with lemon."

He says, "Yes, sir, as you wish. Will there be anything else?"

I say, "No, just the tea and strawberries. Thank you, Chandler."

The tea room is how we refer to the large semi-circular area on the second floor at the rear of the edifice. It faces north away from Cretaceous World and overlooks Tumtum Creek. The entire curved wall of the tea room is made of sheets of shatter-proof glass. They're fitted together so artfully that you can only find the seams if you get close and inspect the surface of the glass very carefully.

Outside, the temperature is 95 degrees Fahrenheit on this mid-afternoon in late May, but the air conditioning keeps it cool and refreshing in here. The half-acre of solar panels on the roof of the residence give us plenty of electricity for all the conveniences we fancy.

I ascend the spiral staircase and make my way to the tea room. I park myself on the antique Stickley couch and gaze out at the dense forest. Red alders and vine maples are leafing out along the creek, as are the oaks up the hillside. The endless pines are green as ever.

Chandler soon brings the tea and strawberries and sets them on the small table in front of me. I enjoy his style and politeness. It's very soothing.

I say, "I'd like to hear the creek, please."

Chandler turns on the sound from Tumtum Creek. A microphone has been hidden at a spot where the rushing water passes over a series of three small waterfalls, none of which is more than a foot high. The gorgeous natural music floods the tea room from surrounding speakers. It's complex and simple at the same time.

Chandler discreetly leaves the room.

I say to myself, "Tumtum," remembering its meaning in the Chinook Jargon: heart, mind, will.

I sip the delicious Earl Grey tea with two lemons fresh-squeezed into the pot. I pick up a luscious strawberry and take a big bite out of it.

I think, "Tumtum. Perfect."

At this moment, Becky appears. She's been to the doctor in New Geneva for her annual checkup.

She quietly says, "Hey."

I answer, "Hey."

I immediately sense something's not right.

She says, "The creek sounds nice."

She says it as if she's remembering how it sounds, not actually hearing it right now.

I ask, "Care for a strawberry?"

I lift the bowl and hold it out to her.

She says, "No, thanks. I don't think I could eat anything right now."

She sits down beside me on the plush maroon couch.

I say, "Tea, then?"

Chandler thoughtfully brought two cups when he delivered the tea.

She says, "No."

I ask, "Something the doctor said?"

She says, "Yeah, you could say that. She definitely said something."

I put my half-eaten strawberry down on a coaster and wait.

She says, "My lab work turned up a problem. They found positive indications for Stander's disease."

I say, "Heard the name. Not familiar."

She explains, "It's a new virus that's come along in the last couple decades, now that the climate's changed so much. It's a kind of dementia accompanied by a physical wasting away. You lose your mind and your body. You lose it all. You lose yourself. You've got two to three years from the time it shows up in the tests to when you're still alive but you're not you anymore."

I don't know what to say. I'm not prepared in any way to deal with this. It's the last thing I was expecting to hear her say.

I say, "You look so healthy. You look so well."

I'm looking at her, and she turns her head and looks at me with her beautiful green eyes. Tears begin to trickle down her cheeks, and I put my arms around her. My own eyes fill with tears and overflow.

I ask, "Is there any doubt about the diagnosis?"

She says, "She's repeating the tests just to make 110 percent sure, but she doesn't hold out any false hope. She says the diagnosis is clear. The lab results are unambiguous."

She utters a single sob, and I hug her harder.

She says, "It's difficult to accept that it's true. It doesn't seem possible."

I agree, "No, it doesn't seem real at all."

She asks, "I'd like to go down by the creek: can we?"

I reply, "Of course."

There's a door off the tea room opening onto stairs down to Tumtum Creek. We're both a bit wobbly as we descend. I hold onto the railing, and Becky holds tightly onto me.

It's muggy outside. The temperature is at least fifteen degrees cooler in the shade down by the creek.

I say, "There's supposed to be a thunderstorm tonight."

She says, "It feels like it."

We stop beside the rushing flow of the creek.

She asks, "Do you ever wish we'd had a child?"

I lie, "No."

She comments, "I suppose this whole place, Cretaceous World, is our child. It's why we're alive. It's our purpose in life."

I agree, "Yes, I suppose it is. I hadn't thought of it that way exactly, but I suppose it's so."

She says, "I'm glad we don't have a child who has to face this, my dying, his or her mother's dying."

I agree, "It would be hard to tell a child."

We're silent thinking about breaking the news to a child we don't have.

She says, "I don't want you to have to face losing your wife before she's actually dead. I don't want to live past the time when I'm still myself."

I ask, "What do you mean?"

She says, "You know what I mean."

I say, "You mean assisted suicide."

She confirms, "Yes, I want to consider it in a year or two when the time comes, when it's obvious that I don't have much longer before I don't know who you are or anything we've done together."

I embrace her.

I say, "Of course. However you want. I'll be with you whatever comes."

She says, "I don't want you to remember me like I'll become if I let it happen. I want you to remember me like this."

We kiss tenderly, and all the love and joy of all our life together is in this kiss.

* * * * * * * * * * *

I'm standing in the tower at night. Lightning flashes and crashes outside the panoramic glass windows.

I think, "Like the late Jurassic."

We have a whole crew of forest workers dedicated to maintaining a 300-yard firebreak around the dinosaur areas. It's in effect a circumambient meadow. Deer graze there. We also have dinosaur-sized, cave-like fire shelters in every area. We humans have our cars and our roads in case we need to flee. There's never been a forest fire here at Cretaceous World, but we're ready for what's probably the inevitable.

The flashing and crashing continue outside the windows of the circular fourth floor.

I suddenly notice I'm not alone. There's a plump, slope-shouldered fellow in a nice suit standing beside me.

He says soothingly, "Never fear, my friend, all is well."

I find I know his name.

I turn toward him and say, "Diablo, my nemesis, what brings you here tonight?"

He winks and says, "You know."

I find I do.

I say, "Becky."

He says, "You find you wish Stander's Disease were an enemy, a villain you could face and kill with a knife-thrust to the navel, do you not?"

He's not wrong.

I say, "When cellular life on Earth began around four billion years ago, immortality was possible. It wasn't until the nucleated protists came along much later that death became inevitable."

He says, "You call me Diablo, but you know I'm really just entropy."

I say, "You're the inevitable death of the Universe."

A titanic bolt of lightning flashes across the sky, and at least fifteen seconds later, a soul-shattering thunder-crack shakes me to my core.

Diablo says soothingly, "Never fear, my friend, all is well."

I say, "The Brontosaurs I saw today will probably live a couple hundred years or more."

By the time I reach the end of that sentence, I'm awake in bed with Becky sleeping soundly beside me.

Her peaceful, heavy breathing goes round and round. I think of a mill wheel going around, driven by the powerful flow of a creek.

DEWBERRY

Sheriff Bob Holmes is sitting at his large wooden desk in the Dewberry Sheriff's Department office on Main Street. As is usually the case here, there's nothing to do, no crimes to solve in the little town or its surroundings, so the sheriff and his Deputy Jimmy Watson are relaxing, chatting, enjoying the long, slow moment. They'll go out on patrol a little later, which won't take very long, and then they'll be back here doing what they're doing now, taking it easy and chewing the fat.

This particular morning, however, Bob finds he has a bone to pick with Jimmy, which leads to a round of the petty squabbling old friends can do without anger or desire to wound.

The sheriff asks, "You taking Melba to the Bijou on Friday night?"

The deputy answers, "Oh, I don't know."

Bob demands, "What do you mean you don't know?"

Jimmy says, "I probably will. You taking Laura?"

Bob says, "I am."

Jimmy says, "Well then, let's go together."

Bob says, "You're kind of taking Melba for granted."

Jimmy objects, "I'm what?"

Bob repeats, "Taking Melba for granted."

Jimmy asks, "Now what makes you say that?"

Bob explains, "You haven't asked her if she wants to go."

Jimmy says, "Well, no, but she'll go."

Bob says it again, "You're taking her for granted."

Jimmy insists, "Am not."

Bob persists, "Are too."

"Am not."

"Are too."

The door to the Sheriff's Department opens, and Alma comes in. She's there to clean the two jail cells, the bathroom, the little back room, the office area itself, the whole general shebang.

She says, "Hello, boys."

They return the greeting.

She goes into the back room and gets the cleaning cart. She wheels it into the first jail cell, which faces the office area. She begins to clean.

Bob returns to his theme, "You're taking a chance, you know."

Jimmy says, "No, I'm not. I'm not taking any chance at all."

Bob warns, "If you keep taking Melba for granted, you may turn around one day and find she's gone."

Jimmy boasts, ignoring the presence of Alma nearby, "Melba is wrapped around my little finger. She's not going anywhere."

Bob scoffs, "Oh, really."

Jimmy repeats, "I've got her wrapped around my little finger. Yes, sir, she's crazy about me."

Bob says, "All right, then. Don't say I didn't warn you."

Jimmy says, "I won't."

Bob says, "Don't come crying to me."

Jimmy says, "Don't worry, I won't."

Bob says, "Wrapped around your little finger, you say."

Jimmy confirms, "That's right. I'll tell her she and I are going to the movies with Laura and you, and she'll say fine."

Bob says, "She'll just say yes, sir."

Jimmy says, "That's what she'll do."

Bob clarifies, "So you'll just say jump, and she'll just ask how high?"

Jimmy insists, "Exactly right."

Bob reminds, "You know, scripture says pride goeth before destruction, and a haughty spirit before a fall."

Jimmy objects, "A man's got to be proud. You know that."

Bob gives up, "Whatever you say, my young friend. Why don't we go get us some doughnuts and coffee and then go on patrol?"

Jimmy likes the sound of that plan. He feels like he won the argument, and doughnuts seem like a fine reward.

Jimmy smiles and says, "Yes, sir, you're the boss."

The sheriff tells Alma to lock up if she leaves before they get back.

Alma tells him not to worry.

The sheriff and deputy put on their sunglasses and step out into the mid-morning heat of June 2117.

Alma immediately gets out her phone and taps in a number.

When Melba answers the call, Alma says, "I just heard something I've got to tell you. It's about Jimmy."

Alma repeats what Jimmy said about having Melba wrapped around his little finger.

Melba is incensed. She says Jimmy needs an attitude adjustment big-time. She promises she'll give him one he'll never forget.

* * * * * * * * * * *

He said, "You're taking her for granted."

That's what he said to his deputy this morning.

Bob is sitting in his lounge chair with the footrest up. The lamp is on beside him. He's at home. It's after midnight, but he can't sleep.

He thinks, "Virginia would've been asleep by now."

He imagines that she's in the bedroom now, sleeping while he stays awake. They used to do that a lot. She'd call him a night owl and laugh as she went off to bed.

He took that for granted. Now that she's been dead a year, it seems a treasured memory to him. It brings tears to his eyes now. He's not a particularly sentimental man, but this he feels deeply, the absence of what he used to take for granted, of her whom he so often, so obliviously had taken for granted.

He remembers sitting through the night beside Virginia's open casket at the funeral home. He'd come straight from work and was still wearing his uniform.

He could see that his hands were trembling. He was dripping sweat even though he felt cold all over, chilled through and through from the inside out. His breathing was labored. He was clenching his teeth to keep them from chattering.

When he went into the bathroom at the funeral home, he looked into the mirror. His face was very pale. He saw an expression of unspeakable terror, pain, and pleading on the face in the mirror. He pulled his service revolver from the holster on his hip and stuck the barrel into his mouth. He continued to look into the mirror as he did this. His finger tightened on the trigger. The hammer just started to pull back into position to snap forward and fire the bullet. Then his finger relaxed. The hammer stopped pulling back and returned to its original position.

He slid the revolver back in the holster on his hip and returned to his seat beside the body of his beloved Virginia. He couldn't bear the thought of dishonoring her death with his own suicide. He wouldn't disgrace her memory that way.

Now a year later, he loves life. It took courage, character, guts to keep on living, but now it's easy.

Now he goes to the movies or the dance at the Grange Hall with Laura and Jimmy and Melba, and he laughs and jokes and spreads joy all around.

The awareness of Virginia's grave in the historic cemetery on the edge of town, the memory of the lovely ceremony there, these never leave him.

Now the joy of being alive is lighter, is hollow at the core. Humor is everywhere he looks, everywhere he is. The absurdity of things never leaves his heart, his mind, his soul. His words flow like a babbling brook from the vast clouds of inscrutability that rain intermittent mystery on the metaphoric mountains of existence.

These days Bob sometimes says, "I used to know what was what. Now I don't know a thing."

* * * * * * * * * * *

The next morning, Jimmy is late for work. His eyes are red, like he's been crying, and the skin under his eyes is darkened, like he hasn't gotten much sleep, if any.

The sheriff says, "Morning, Jim."

The deputy says glumly, "Morning."

The sheriff asks, "Rough night?"

Jimmy moans, "You could say that."

Bob says, "Sorry to hear it. Melba didn't feel like jumping, I take it."

Jimmy says, "Huh? Oh yeah. No, she didn't. No, she didn't."

Bob shakes his head in sympathy.

Jimmy demands, "Did you say anything to her?"

Bob assures him, "Nothing. I wouldn't do that. You know that."

Jimmy follows up, "Did you say anything to anybody about what I said about Melba yesterday?"

Bob protests, "Of course not. You know me better than that."

Jimmy says mournfully, "Well, someone sure did."

Bob suggests, "Alma."

Jimmy says, "Alma?"

Bob elaborates, "She was cleaning the jail cell right over there. Remember? She heard the last part of what you said. You know, the part about wrapping around little fingers."

Jimmy wails, "Alma. I was so wrapped up in what I was arguing that I forgot all about her."

Bob scolds, "Jimmy, you've lived in Dewberry your whole life, same as me. You know that anything you say is going to be heard by everyone before long. If you don't want everyone who lives here to hear something, don't say it to anybody."

Jimmy repeats, "Alma. Alma told Melba. Sure she did."

Bob agrees, "Seems like it."

Jimmy pleads, "You've got to help me. Please. What do I do? Melba's so mad. She says it's over. She says for me to leave her alone, to go away and never come back, to steer clear of her for forever."

Bob suggests, "To hit the road, Jim? To darken her doorstep no more?"

Jimmy protests, "You're not helping. Please. I need your help. I don't know what to do now."

Bob explains, "Well, there's only the one thing for you to do in these current circumstances."

He pauses.

Jimmy starts to blurt but resists the impulse.

Bob notices and smiles in appreciation.

Finally though, Jimmy erupts, "What? What is it?"

Bob says, "Apologize, beg, grovel, crawl, throw yourself on her mercy, plead for forgiveness, make her pity you, show her how important she is to your happiness, to your sanity really, convince her you'll never do it again, never ever."

Jimmy becomes quiet and finally just murmurs, "Oh."

Bob says, "There isn't any other way. You can keep your pride, or you can get your girlfriend back. You can't do both."

Jimmy moans, "Oh, man."

Bob advises, "Do whatever you have to do to get Melba back. You two kids are made for each other. You're not going to find another like her. I can tell you from personal experience how valuable that is."

Jimmy groans, "I don't know if I can do it."

Bob encourages, "Sure you can. Now get on out there and grovel, beg, apologize, promise to be good from now on. Go on, you can do it."

Jimmy shuffles grimly out the door.

The sheriff thinks, "How will it end. I wonder."

ILLAHEE

enjoy standing on the train platform, pretending I'm just a visitor.

The woman beside me says to her two young boys, "The train's almost here. It won't be much longer."

A train comes by every stop once an hour here at Cretaceous World. She asks them, "Which dinosaur do you want to see first?"

They both cry, "T-rex! T-rex!"

I offer, "You know, the Spinosaur is even bigger, and some people think it's scarier."

She says, "Thanks, but they've been dying to see T-rex for a long time. I already knew what they'd say."

She smiles. I smile. The boys are quiet. I like to think they're considering this new information about the Spinosaur.

There are about two hundred people on the platform here by the entrance to the park. It's approaching ten a.m. on a Wednesday in August 2117, and the temperature outside will probably hit more than 120 degrees later today. It's nice and cool here inside the train station though, and it will stay that way. There are people of all ages and several races gathered together to take this ride into the Mesozoic past. I hear German being spoken from somewhere near me. Japanese too. And French. No one suspects I'm anything other than a visitor just like they are. Nobody guesses I'm sort of the de facto king of this sprawling realm of a dinosaur park. I see it as my duty to move around the twenty mile by thirty mile territory every day and see first-hand how the many and varied facets of its daily operation are functioning.

The train system is really more of a subway. The ten stations are aboveground, but the rest of the nearly fifty miles of track is underground. More buried, really, than underground. We didn't want the track and the trains to be visible or audible, so we put a concrete shell over them and covered it with dirt that soon had grass and brush growing on it. Onto the topmost part of the miles-long serpentine berm, thousands of solar panels have been placed to power the train system including the trains themselves.

The ten o'clock train pulls into the main station right on time, and its passengers deboard from its several cars. Then all of us who have been waiting step on board and find a place.

Once I'm seated, my attention is drawn to a solitary old man who's sitting with his back to the window. He looks a lot like me physically. He looks lonely. I imagine a past for him. I imagine he failed to take a chance forty years ago, failed to make a declaration to a woman, and now he's living out his final years all alone, somber and disappointed through all his remaining days. No, that's not it. Of course, it isn't. He did make the declaration to the special woman, did love her body and soul and was loved by her, but then she died. After decades of life and love together, she fell ill and died. Of what, exactly, it doesn't matter. She's gone, and he's alone. That's what matters.

I fear facing Becky's long slow decline. I feel ashamed of my self-pity and fight it, but it keeps coming back. Stander's Disease is relentless. Wasting away. Dementia. I show my love to her and hide my aversion, but I fear she senses the truth. She's set on assisted suicide when the final phase begins, and I know it's as much for my sake as her own, that it's an expression of her love for me and her desire not to watch me watching her gruesome ordeal. She wants to go quickly and gracefully and not spoil the memory of what we've had together.

The train halts at the first stop, which is where the Hadrosaurs are. There are ten stops in all, each several miles apart. This includes the Main Station plus one stop each for the nine kinds of dinosaurs we have: the Iguanodons at Station 2, the Ankylosaurs at Station 3, Stegosaurs at Station 4, and continuing in sequence, the Pachycephalosaurs, the pair of Triceratops, the Brontosaurs, the T-rex couple, the Spinosaurs. The parallel sets of track wind side by side among the nine dinosaur areas. When a train reaches the far end, it goes around a short, tight loop and returns on the parallel set of track back the way it came. It takes each of the half dozen trains three full hours to run the entire route from Main Station to far end and back, making all the stops along the way.

It isn't easy or fast getting around the park. It requires commitment from the visitor. We put computer games for the kids at each station, but we expect the adults to stop their own rushing around and just think while they wait for a dinosaur or a train to show up. The guidebook we give them as part of the price of admission provides lots of basic facts about the nine pairs of dinosaurs, about the way our genomic technicians have re-created them, and about the Mesozoic in general. This is really the purpose of this place: to spread awareness and understanding of the history of life on Earth.

Becky and I like to ask each other, "What do you think this is: an amusement park?"

And we laugh every time as if we've never heard the joke before.

When the train stops at Station 4, some of us get up and exit.

I recognize the security guard by the entrance to the viewing area and say, "Hi, Jerry. How's it going today?"

He brightens and says, "Good. Good."

He's a middle-aged fellow in excellent shape. We have a lot of security guards, and they all train together in the Aikido dojo by the bunkhouse. It's a requirement of their employment that they do this. No guns, just Aikido: that's our policy. We give them more pay and better benefits than any police officers in Oregon get. We hardly ever lose one to another job somewhere else.

The viewing area is about a hundred yards long and has lots of padded benches in front of the glass wall that faces toward the Stegosaurs. All nine of the viewing areas are essentially luxurious, attractive, air-conditioned cages for humans, and this spot is no exception. There's no way for someone to get outside and try to enter the dinosaur area.

The Stegosaur pen is the smallest one, only a little over two miles square. This is because Stegosaurs are quite slow-moving and don't roam around very much. Their top speed is about three miles an hour. The femur is significantly longer than the tibia in a Stegosaur leg, and they don't really run but just kind of shuffle. They also have a tiny brain, hence very little curiosity. They don't feel the need to explore. If they have enough to eat, they're happy just to be there like a cow in a field.

We're up about a hundred feet high on a naturally elevated part of the hilly terrain and can look down over the big crane to see where several tons of maidenhair ferns and brackens have been dumped into the pen. I stop and gaze down, and there they are, the two Stegosaurs, happily munching away.

The first thing you notice is the alternating double row of plates along the spine. The largest plates are at the hips, tapering toward the head and tail. Each high, wide plate stands up vertically and has a point on its upper end. They're honeycombed with cavities and are no thicker than a man's arm. Blood circulates through the vessels that line the outer surfaces of the plates, and this helps to heat and cool the ectothermic Stegosaurs. If they stand in the sun, the blood vessels on their plates are heated rapidly, and if they stand in the shade, the heat dissipates rapidly via these same vessels. These plates can also blush to express sexual desire, which is probably why they only develop in adulthood.

These blithely grazing creatures are thirty feet long and weigh 5,000 pounds. They're sturdy, low to the ground, and have two pairs of spikes sticking out sideways from their tail-tips. A blow from one of those spiked tails could take out the leg of an attacking Allosaur and leave it limping off or lying helpless on the bloody ground.

Unlike the Brontosaur that just swallows its food without chewing and then grinds it up with rocks in its digestive track, the Stegosaur has cheeks and chews with teeth positioned at the rear of its sharply beaked mouth. The cheeks keep all the foliage and fructifications from falling out while it peacefully munches away. I like the cheeks for some reason.

The most powerful part of a Stegosaur's tiny brain is the olfactory area. They can smell really well. My academic specialization is in microbiology, especially in bacteria, and my study of single-celled beings tells me that smell is the most ancient of all the senses. Bacteria can sense chemical changes around themselves, basically smell them, then determine the presence of danger or food from that. Those non-nucleated single cells have no brain at all, yet they perform many cognitive functions, both individually and collectively. It interests me that this dinosaur with the teensy brain also relies on its keen sense of smell to survive and thrive.

Given the gloomy medical outlook for my dear wife, I can't help but envy the Stegosaurs for being unable to think of the future. I can't help but wish I too had a tiny, futureless brain, or better yet, no more brain than a bacterium.

I feel a vibrating on my thigh and pull my personal communicator out of my pocket.

I find a new message on it that says, "Return to residence ASAP. Urgent."

* * * * * * * * * * * * *

When I reached the residence, the Sheriff of Dewberry was wait-ing. Chandler met me at the front door as usual and said, "Sheriff Holmes is in the reception room."

Something wasn't usual about the way he spoke. I looked at him quizzically, and he just looked into the distance.

I went to the reception room and opened the door. The sheriff was sitting inside.

I said, "Hello, Bob. Good to see you."

He just said, "Hello, Ted."

Something wasn't usual about the way the sheriff spoke either.

I can't bear to remember the exact words he said to me next. Stand-ing here in the cemetery five days later, I can't abide those words.

Their meaning was that my dear wife Becky was dead.

Becky had driven into New Geneva to see a specialist about the progress of her disease. She was coming home from the doctor's office, going west on Highway 137, when an eastbound drunk driver had let his big pickup drift across the center line of the two-lane road and smash head-on into her little coupe. The sheriff didn't tell me that the air bag had knocked her unconscious and that she had bled out from deep cuts to her left leg and arm. I learned this later. The point was: she was dead, Becky was dead, the love of my life was dead.

The sheriff sat there, waiting to see how I was going to react. I managed to keep it together long enough for him to do his duty and leave. He was a decent person and a good friend to Cretaceous World. The tourists who flocked year-round to our dinosaur park were the economic mainstay of his adjacent town. Becky and I had known him for years and liked him well enough. It probably helped his attitude to-wards us that we'd always made sizeable contributions to his re-election campaigns.

The funeral for Becky was this morning, five days later, at 8:00 a.m. when the temperature in the shade would still be below 90 degrees. I've stayed behind after everyone else has left, except for the clean-up crew loading folding chairs onto a truck. This little cemetery was cre-ated by Becky. She gave it its name, Illahee Haven, because it sits be-side the Illahee River. All the creeks in Cretaceous World flow into the Illahee, which runs along the park's western boundary, miles away from where the tourists are. She liked the word "illahee," Chinook Jargon for land, region, home.

The ceremony today was nice enough. An old friend from the

Religious Studies Department at SUNG gave a proper eulogy. Hundreds of employees from Cretaceous World attended, even though it wasn't at all obligatory. No pressure at all. They just came because they wanted to honor her. Many citizens of Dewberry also attended, including Sheriff Holmes and his two deputies. Becky really was loved by everyone in our little world. Like me, she was an only child. She's 66, three years younger than I, and like mine, her parents passed away some time ago, so neither she nor I had any family left to attend her funeral.

Randy Winston, the trillionaire founder and funder of Cretaceous World, flew in on his private jet, which he left at the airport in New Geneva and arrived at the cemetery this morning in a big black limo. Before he headed over to Dewberry a short while ago to have a pancake breakfast at the Hominid's Delight, he offered me his condolences and said he wanted to talk with me in a week or so. I knew what he meant. We'd have to work out who was going to take over Becky's duties at the park.

Lana Gable hung around and was among the last to leave. She came over to me right after Randy drove off.

She said, "I'm so sorry. Becky was a wonderful woman."

I thanked her.

She said, "How are you holding up? Are you all right?"

I said I was fine.

She said, "Well, let me know if there's anything I can do to help."

I said I would.

She hugged me, smiled at me, and turned to go.

I watched her blonde ponytail bounce as she walked away.

Now I'm alone. Even the work crew has driven off with their load of folding chairs.

I go down to the riverbank. I find a big smooth rock beside the Illahee and sit down on it.

I say to Becky, "So here you are now. Here you are."

I begin to sob and can't stop. The sound of my wailing mingles with the steady murmur of the flowing Illahee.

* * * * * * * * * * * *

It's the day after the funeral, and I'm making the soup of life. That's the name I gave to the soup Becky invented to keep me healthy, wealthy, and wise. She fed it to me every day, and I'm sure it's a big reason why I'm in such good health for a geezer. She herself preferred a giant bowl of salad every day. I named that the big salad. I don't care for salad, so I eat the soup of life instead.

Suddenly, she's not here to make it for me. We have a chef here at the grand residence, but Becky always made it for me. She knew I would want to make it myself if she weren't around, so she left me detailed instructions how to do that. Just reading the sentences, I can feel the way her mind worked and hear her voice. I feel her beside me, pressed close against me.

The ingredients give you everything you need: water, onion, celery, carrots, potatoes, quinoa, lima beans, green beans, shelled edamame, black-eyed peas, green peas, sweet corn, spinach, brown rice.

This is an example of her precise written directions: "Depending on the volume of vegetables, sometimes there is more soup than the stockpot can hold. When that's the case, split the soup between two pots before adding spinach. Using a glass four-cup (one-quart) measuring cup, transfer four quarts of soup to a six-quart Dutch oven in order to make room for stirring in the spinach. Add one package of spinach to the Dutch oven and two packages of spinach to the larger stock pot. Stir."

And so forth. Her single-spaced instructions continue for three full pages.

I read her words aloud now. I feel very close to her when I do this. I keep bursting into tears. I feel her presence with me so definitely.

I think of Cybil and Clyde. Those are the nicknames the crew gave to the pair of Stegosaurs. I'm glad now that I don't have a brain the size of a walnut like Cybil and Clyde do. I'm glad I can think ahead and foresee losing the vividness of dear Becky's memory. I can choose to resist that, to keep feeling her presence beside me. I can choose not to let her fade away.

Sometimes something happens that makes apparent the strangeness of ordinary reality. I look around myself here in this sprawling kitchen with its shiny double-wide stainless-steel refrigerator and its rows of handsome maple cabinets and its beautiful red-and-gold tile floor and find it all strange. How utterly weird is this polished pink marble slab on this kitchen island and this medium onion which I'm chopping up into small bits with this big sharp knife. How eerie it is that these vegetables have arrived through history from various continents and more recently from many local farms and some not so local to sit here beside each other on these lovely countertops, waiting to mingle with each other and become the soup of life in my pot and last for days in separate serving-sized containers in my refrigerator and for weeks in my huge freezer. How bizarre it is that the zillion cells of my body and the even more numerous bacteria in my gut can digest and derive nourishment from these once-living beings.

I remember how Becky and I would pretend that she wasn't sick, that nothing was wrong, that everything would be just fine. If the two of us agreed about that, then we could make it seem true. I don't have the power to do that all by myself.

I embrace this ordinary strangeness now. I want to feel the uneasiness it brings. I want to be alive, absurdly holding tight the memory, no, the wondrous presence here beside me so palpably, of Rebecca Beebe, my dear wife, the love of my life.

FOUNDER

Randy says, "We'd best get down to business before my many fans show up."

He flashes a big smile to suggest he likes the adulation but would rather get things done.

Ted says, "We've got about twenty minutes, if past behavior is any guide."

The two men have just been seated at the big table in the back corner where Randy likes it best. He can see everybody and everything that's happening in the restaurant from there.

It's August 2117, about a week after the funeral of Ted's beloved wife Becky.

As they sit there, the word is going out all around the little mountain town of Dewberry: Randy Winston is in the Hominid's Delight!

Soon the mayor, the school principal, the local doctor, the owner of the general store, the postmaster, and other notable citizens will show up to have brunch alongside the founder and funder of Cretaceous World, whether they're hungry or not. Randy's the person who put Dewberry on the map, who transformed the tiny town from a benighted backwater into a thriving resort destination, and local residents revere him as modern Dewberry's de facto founding father.

Randy says to Ted, "Becky's passing has left a big hole in our operation."

Ted nods, "In my heart too."

Randy asks, "How are you holding up? Do you need any help coping with it? I can fly in a really good shrink, the best, if that will do you any good."

Ted assures his old friend, "No need. I'm handling it."

The waitress shows up to take their order, and Randy asks her to come back in twenty minutes.

Randy tells Ted, "I'd better just ask you what you recommend. How do you think we should proceed?"

Ted says, "Well, you're right, as usual: I do have a plan. I've been thinking Lana Gable would be excellent to put in place as the general manager of the park. She's a PhD in paleontology and has an expert knowledge of our dinosaurs. She likes living here and gets along with all the staff members. She's a pied piper: she plays her flute, and they all gladly follow wherever she leads."

Randy says, "I take it you too like working with her."

Ted confirms, "I do."

Randy says, "That's as important to me as any of the other considerations."

Ted proposes, "I think we should offer her the job."

Randy says, "All right. Talk with her and see if she wants the job. If she does, send me a detailed description of her duties, you know, a formal document I can file away and feel like we followed a good process. I trust your judgment about the park implicitly. You've built this place from a daydream to an amazing reality that's famous the world over."

Ted smiles, "Thanks, I appreciate your saying that."

Randy says, "I mean it too. I never tell people I admire and trust them unless I do. The secret to my success in all my businesses is that I recognize competence in key people, empower them, put them in leadership positions, and then get completely the hell out of their way."

Ted says, "I know. You're the ideal employer. You really are."

Randy asks, "So, does that cover it? Anything else we need to talk about?"

Ted replies, "There is. I'd like to hire a real director for the museum. I'd like to expand it and turn it into one of the important fossil museums in the world."

Randy brightens, "Really? It's a brilliant idea! I love it."

Ted warns, "It won't be cheap. It will take a boatload of dollars to do it right, and I know you won't want to do it unless we do it right."

Randy smiles and leans back, "Don't worry about the money. The first billion is the hardest. Now the billions just keep piling up faster than I can spend them."

Ted comments, "I admire how you spend lavishly but never throw money away."

Randy nods in agreement, "Yes, people often just look at the scale of spending in my projects and don't get how much I hate wasting money."

Ted smiles, "It's an amazing combination, really."

Randy says, "So write the description of the museum director position and send it to me. Go ahead and start the national search. I'll check in with you as you move ahead in the process."

Ted beams, "I'm pleased, very pleased."

Randy asks, "That it? Should we order now?"

Ted says, "That's it. Let's eat."

Randy waves to the waitress, who has been watching attentively. She comes right over to the table, and the two old friends place their order.

Their timing has been good. Right after the waitress leaves, the first of the fans of Randy arrives.

* * * * * * * * * * * *

Ted and Randy met some fifty years ago when they were undergraduates at the University of Southern California. They lived in the same dorm on campus and were roommates by the time they were sophomores. Ted was a biology major and spent his time in the science buildings. Randy was a double major in business administration and electrical engineering. Their paths crossed often on the compact, focused campus. It was back at the dorm though that they loved to talk of ideas and dreams.

Randy always had a way of thinking outside the rules. He saw possibilities Ted just didn't see. This difference in perception manifested itself on all scales from huge to tiny, from long-term to momentary. Ted likes to remember the time Randy showed him how to slip past the obstacles to using the deluxe weight room just down the street from their dorm.

Randy asked him, "You want to go lift weights with the football players?"

Ted objected, "They won't let us in there. It's players only."

Randy explained, "Well, yeah, but players of any sport. We're tall. We can say we're sand-court volleyball players."

Ted shook his head, "I don't know. I doubt it will work. I don't think I can pull it off."

Randy assured him, "Oh, it will work. I've already done it once. It was only a few days ago. Just let me do all the talking."

Ted opened his eyes wide, "You did this? You haven't said anything about it."

Randy said, "I just did. It hadn't come up yet, and now it has. Come on. Get into your gym clothes, and let's go."

So they went over to the splendid gym facilities that the gifted athletes of the legendary football team used. As Randy had said, other varsity athletes could use the exclusive gym area too, but the demigods of the gridiron dominated the place.

Randy instructed, "Remember, let me do the talking. Just act like you belong there and know what you're doing."

So Ted followed Randy the few blocks over to the forbidden inner sanctum where the capability for national football glory was cultivated, and in they went. Not that they needed to be there. The equipment in the ordinary gym was entirely adequate for their humble needs. Being in the presence of so much size and talent though, it did expand one's sense of what was possible. That's what Randy was looking for, and Ted liked following along, having his horizons expanded too.

A couple years later during the spring semester of their senior year, the two good friends made a fateful excursion just across the street from their dorm. They lived at the intersection of Exposition Boulevard and Vermont Avenue on the southwest corner of the USC campus.

One Saturday morning, Randy said to Ted, "I'm thinking I'd like to walk over now to the Dinosaur Hall at the museum in Exposition Park. We're almost out of here, and I really want to see that before we go."

Ted said, "Excellent idea. I'm definitely up for that."

So off they went. They crossed the boulevard at the light and sauntered the short distance to the Natural History Museum of Los Angeles County.

Randy proposed as they stood before the Triceratops fossil, "We ought to build one of those."

Ted replied, "Someone sure should."

Randy pursued, "You and I, we should do it."

Ted laughed softly, "Okay, sure, we'll build a Triceratops."

Randy expanded, "Someday let's hire some geneticists who can engineer genomes and have them make a living copy of this. I want to see one of these alive, running, snorting, chewing food, and whatever else it did."

Ted asked, "Why stop at one? If one's good, why wouldn't more be even better? These beauties used to roam in great numbers across the landscape of seventy million years ago."

Randy considered, "Great numbers? Hmmm. Let's just make a couple of them and put them on some land in a wet, green place up north somewhere."

Ted approved, "We should absolutely do that. Why limit ourselves to just a couple Triceratops though? Why not a couple T-rex too?"

The two friends strolled over to the trio of T-rex fossils there in the Dinosaur Hall.

Randy agreed, "We'll definitely need some T-rex copies too."

Ted pointed out, "That's going to cost a pretty penny. One of us better make a fortune to pay for our dinosaurs. It'll have to be you, I'm afraid. I don't see a fortune in my future."

Randy affirmed, "I can do that. No problem. I was planning on that anyway."

Ted envisioned, "We'll build a giant dinosaur park with many kinds of dinosaurs. We'll call the place Cretaceous World. People will come from far and wide to see the Triceratops, the T-rex, and all the others."

Randy beamed, "I like it. Yes, let's definitely do that. I hereby hire you as the permanent CEO of Cretaceous World and agree to pay any and all costs for building and running the place."

* * * * * * * * * * * *

The mayor and her husband enter the Hominid's Delight. The waitress meets them and shows them to their table. The mayor leaves her purse on her chair and comes over to see Randy, her husband trailing amiably behind her.

Randy and the mayor exchange pleasantries.

The school principal enters the restaurant with his wife. They take a table and come over to see Randy.

Randy and the principal exchange pleasantries.

The Justice of the Peace enters, takes a table, and comes over.

Randy and the judge exchange pleasantries.

The local doctor enters, takes a table, comes over, and exchanges pleasantries.

The owner of the general store enters, takes a table, comes over, exchanges pleasantries.

The young postmaster enters with two elderly retirees. There's only one empty table left, and even though they've come to the restaurant separately, the three agree to share it.

The postmaster doesn't come over to exchange pleasantries with Randy but does wave and smile at him. The two retirees just watch the visiting celebrity with ingenuous curiosity.

After Randy's admirers have all seated themselves at their tables, the waitress brings Randy's and Ted's food. The two men are quite hungry and eat with enthusiasm. The audience looks on approvingly.

Randy pauses and says to Ted, "Living the dream, my old friend, living the dream."

Ted winks and grins, "As good as it gets. Just like you said it would be."

HORNS

I say, "The Triceratops is so horny today."

She says, "The Triceratops are always horny."

She smiles, and her eyes twinkle.

I just mean the animal I'm looking at down there in the pen is part of the strangeness I feel everywhere now that dear Becky is dead. Lana means some sort of double entendre, I'm pretty sure.

I let it go and just look at both the Triceratops, Bonnie and Lloyd, which is what we call them. They're peacefully munching on a couple tons of Gunnera and Cycad fronds that Lana has had Bud drop into the Triceratops area using the giant crane.

I'm fascinated by the way the beaks at the front slice and the teeth at the back chop inside the cheeks. The heads are huge, over eight feet from tip of beak to top of neck shield.

I say, "The owner and I had a meeting, and I need to talk with you about something."

She's surprised and asks, "Mr. Winston had a meeting with you about me?"

I reply, "It ended up being about you. I'd like to talk with you about it up at the residence. Could you come up there this afternoon after you're done feeding the animals?"

She looks amazed, excited, and maybe a little anxious. She, of course, agrees.

I stay behind after she drives off with Bud to feed the Pachycephalosaurs.

It's late morning toward the end of August, and the temperature is already over a hundred degrees. The Triceratops area is shady though, with lots of the big pine trees that have replaced the Douglas firs over the course of the past hundred years. The Triceratops lived in riparian forests toward the end of the Cretaceous, 68 million years ago and thereabouts, when temperatures were similar to this.

I love watching them. They're so contented.

Thirty feet long, standing ten feet tall at the shoulders and weighing ten thousand pounds, they can run over twenty miles per hour. This is why their pen is so big, ten miles by seven miles. They could easily outrun a T-rex. I suspect that the marks of T-rex teeth on fossil Triceratops' bones were made when a T-rex found a Triceratops who was already dead from old age, disease, or whatever and drove off any competing scavengers. Even if it couldn't have just outrun a T-rex, which it could but if for some reason it couldn't, its two long brow-horns could be driven into the carnivore's leg, crippling the slow bipedal predator. A simple charge by a five-ton Triceratops could break the knee or ankle of a T-rex and knock it over. There's a reason why the Triceratops were among the most numerous dinosaurs ever to live.

The neck shield is impressive. It made it hard to get a clean bite on the back of the neck. It also made for impressive display to intimidate rivals or attract mates, plus it also made it easy for them to identify each other as members of the same species.

I like to imagine the many Triceratops that roamed what is now Montana, Wyoming, Colorado, the Dakotas, Alberta, and Saskatchewan. Though they were numerous, there aren't monotypic bone-beds of their remains, so they probably didn't move in herds. They just passed each other in the woods and continued on about their business, possibly challenging each other or mating occasionally.

I ponder the three horns on each beast, two arcing forward from the brows plus a short one on the nose. The bone core of each is covered in hard horn with a pointed tip.

I repeat Lana's words out loud, "The Triceratops are always horny." Very funny.

* * * * * * * * * * * *

I leave the Triceratops area and return to the residence. I don't have much capacity for work these days. I just have to trust that our people will keep doing a superb job even though I'm barely keeping tabs and, of course, Becky not at all.

The way home is familiar: the subway station near the main gate, the parking structure, the restaurant, the gift shop, up past the museum of fossils, the bunkhouse, the headquarters, the plant. It doesn't seem familiar though. Nothing does now.

The residence looks like a palace in a fairy tale. Cinderella might have gone to a ball there and met a prince last night. I wouldn't be surprised to find a glass slipper on the walkway up to the massive double doorway.

Chandler greets me at the entrance, "Welcome home, sir."

These words do seem familiar and comforting. I'm so grateful for them.

I bow slightly and say, "Thanks, Chandler. I'm heading up to the tea room. I'd like a bowl of sliced fresh peaches and a pot of Earl Grey with lemon, please."

He says, "Yes, sir, as you wish. Will there be anything else?"

I say, "Just that Lana Gable will be coming here in the late afternoon. Please show her to the reception room and let me know she's here."

He says, "Certainly, sir."

I take the spiral staircase up to the second floor and go to the semicircular tea room overlooking Tumtum Creek. I take a seat on the Stickley couch and listen to the living sounds of the creek over the sound system. The tea and peaches arrive soon, and I enjoy them while gazing at the alders and vine maples along the creek and the pines on the hillsides.

I think, "All alone. I'm all alone. Still."

I say, "All alone."

I finish the sweet, ripe peach slices and take my second cup of tea with me to the creek. I stop beside the rushing flow. I sip the tea.

I think, "This is where Becky told me she wanted to die before dementia took away her memory, her self."

I say, "I love you."

I feel her presence beside me. I'm sure she's here with me at creekside.

I sit on the grass and take off my shoes. I dangle my bare feet in the cold flow of the creek water. The desire to dangle them instead in warm water, to plunge my whole body in warm water and swim through its warmth, arrives not all that gradually.

I go back up the outside stairs and through the door to the tea room. I pour the rest of the tea into my cup and go up to the third floor. I sip the tea until it's gone. I change into my swimming trunks and go down the hall to the pool. I dive in and swim several laps. I stop in the five-foot water at the shallow end and stand still.

I roar like Roger the T-rex.

I listen to the answering silence.

I say, "If I were a Spinosaur, I'd take you out to deeper water."

I know she's here.

I get out of the pool and dry off with the big fluffy towel. I walk down to our bedroom and take a long, hot shower. I dress in casual clothes.

I call Chandler, "I'll be napping in our bedroom for a little while. Please let me know when Lana arrives."

Chandler says, "Yes, sir. Should I be persistent if you don't respond immediately?"

I chuckle, "Yes, just keep your finger on the intercom buzzer until I give evidence I've returned to the living."

I lie down on the emperor-size bed and drift into sweet sleep. I'm back in the pool again, embracing Becky in the five-foot water, holding her with her head up above the surface, gazing into her luminous, enchanting green eyes.

After that, darkness.

When I wake up, I look at the clock on the nightstand. I was out cold for an hour. I get up and step into the bathroom. I'm barefoot and like the feel of the cool tiles beneath my feet. I wash my face and run a comb through my hair.

I buzz Chandler on the intercom, "I'm up and moving to the tower now. Same deal there: let me know when Lana comes."

I climb the small spiral stairs that go directly from the bedroom to the circular room on the floor above. I admire as ever the panoramic view afforded by the glass walls. I go to the recliner sofa at the center of the tower's circle and sit down. Soon a thought arrives.

I think, "The bitter repeated experience of individuals in civilized society teaches that every intimacy, in the beginning lending life such pleasing diversity and presenting itself as a nice and easy adventure, will most often grow into a major task, extremely complicated, until the situation finally becomes burdensome. Natural desire usually leads to a complicated situation that's hard to resolve and that won't go away anytime soon."

I say, "What do you think this is: an amusement park?"

I'm sure I feel her beside me, laughing at that.

The intercom buzzes, and Chandler lets me know that Lana has arrived.

I don't feel like walking on any more stairs for a while, so I take the elevator that runs from the basement to the tower. You have to have a special security key to get above the second floor.

The reception room is at the front of the first floor. You enter through the grand doors and turn right, continuing just past the great spiral of the central staircase. The room has a lovely view down the hill toward the entrance to the park.

I find Lana sitting there. I see she's stopped off at the bunkhouse and changed out of her work clothes. She's wearing a short skirt and a stretchy top with a little cleavage. She looks very nice, which makes me angry for some reason.

I pause a moment and focus on that unjustified flash of anger. I realize that Lana's attractiveness feels like it pulls me away from Becky. I look at those graceful, smooth legs and feel Becky's presence beside me fading a bit. The sense of losing her threatens me. My hind-brain reacts with ancient fear that expresses itself as irrational anger.

She stares at me with a puzzled look.

I say, "I'm sorry. I was thinking of something else. How are you?"

She says, "Fine. Excited really. I'm flattered to find out Mr. Winston was talking with you about me."

I say, "Yes, well, the situation is this: we need someone to assume Becky's duties here at Cretaceous World. I can't handle things by myself. We think you're the best person for the job. You understand the way the park works from the ground up. You grew up helping to run a ranch. You have an actual degree in paleontology, which neither Becky nor I have. We just had to apply our training in microbiology and botany to learn about dinosaurs and the Cretaceous. Your ability to communicate with people and supervise them effectively is impressive. The position is yours if you want it. It will pay five times what you're making now. A large apartment here in the residence will be provided for you. An office and an assistant will also be yours. Your title will be Executive Director. Does this sound like something you want to do?"

She appears stunned.

She quickly collects herself and says, "I feel like I just won the lottery. Yes, of course I want the position. It sounds fantastic."

I smile, "Okay, you're hired then."

We shake hands and sit down again.

She promises, "You won't regret it, sir. I'll make you glad you gave me this chance."

It's hard not to like Lana.

I mention, "You'll need to find your own replacement. Will you want to hire from within or do a regional or even international search?"

She ponders a few moments, "I'd like to do a search but encourage people already here to apply. It's important to find someone who will like the life here in the park. That's as important as the subject knowledge or practical skills. I'll write a job description right away and give it to you for suggestions and approval."

I feel very pleased.

I say, "You'll need to go to the headquarters tomorrow morning and have Human Resources do the paperwork for your salary and benefits. I'll tell them to be ready for you bright and early. Can Bud fill in for you while you're finding your replacement?"

She says he can.

I add, "I'll also contact the plant and have them round up a moving team to get you moved in here at the residence tomorrow afternoon. Sound good?"

She beams, "Sounds perfect!"

She leaves, and I sense a threshold has been crossed.

* * * * * * * * * * * *

After dinner, I go take a look at Becky's office. If I'm going to show it to Lana, I'd better familiarize myself with it again. I didn't really go in there very often. It was Becky's domain, though I doubt she'd have minded if I did come around.

It's on the second floor, more or less right above the reception area and has the same charming view down the hill, except from a slightly higher viewpoint.

The housekeeper's cart is parked in the hallway next door down, so I step over to that room to let her know that I'll be in Becky's office awhile.

I say, "Eva, …"

She's startled and jumps a little.

She says, "Oh, it's you, Mr. Beebe. I wasn't expecting anyone."

I say, "Sorry. I didn't mean to scare you. I just wanted to tell you I'm going to be in the office next door for a couple hours or so. I hope that won't interfere with your schedule."

She considers briefly, "It's no problem. I'll just work down the hall and come back when you've gone."

I say, "Good. Should I come tell you when I'm done with the room?"

She shakes her head, "No, no, you don't need to do that. I won't come back for several hours."

I don't think she wants to be startled by me again.

I go in the office, closing the door behind me. I stand in the center of the room and look around.

I have a strange feeling and am not inclined to censor myself: I just say words that convey the feeling. Or think them. I hear them loud and clear in my mind.

I think, "I hear a music communicating the union of human existence with primordial Nature, or more precisely a night-music uniting human perception with the no-mind of Nature: we too are the Universe and see that the essence of creation is to express divine love, the Spirit that embraces and nurtures all things."

The silence ripples around me. My mind is the pebble dropped into the pond.

I start looking into drawers. I turn on Becky's computer and see what's in her files. She always shared her passwords with me. It's easy to remember them because they're always either "dino2112" or "2112dino."

I've heard about people who left secrets behind that loved ones found *post mortem*. I don't find anything like that. No secrets. Becky was who she seemed to be.

Going through her files and records makes me feel very close to her. Every little detail adds to the particularity and concreteness of her existence. She seems less like a generalization and more like a specific presence I can reach out and touch.

I still take the erectile pills. I like to maintain the potency to respond at moments like this when I feel her vividly there.

I lock the door and imagine. She's young again, Lana's age more or less. I lift Becky up out of her chair and turn her around, facing away from me. I bend her over her desk and lift her skirt. I imagine that I asked her not to wear anything under her skirt and that she didn't. I slide into her from behind.

I walk into the small bathroom in her office and grab a couple tissues. In my mind, I'm still out at her desk, probing her luscious derriere. I turn her around and have her kneel. I grab her head and hair with both hands and push Theodore into her throat. That's the name she lovingly gave my horn. I relieve myself of my salty load with great pleasure. She swallows it and licks Theodore clean. She's smiling up at me. We're so close. We're one soul.

I say, "Triceratops are always horny."

She laughs so innocently.

DOJO

Larissa finishes her class at the dojo. She's a tenth-dan black belt and is the sensei leading the training session this evening. Tonight she has focused on ushironage, a technique where you guide an aggressive assault slightly past you, deftly circle behind the attacker, and bring both your hands down hard on his or her shoulders, compressing the vertebrae and driving the attacker into and onto the ground. It's a very powerful technique, and care must be taken not to damage the spine of your training partner. In the case of an actual attack outside the dojo, ushironage could easily lead to a crippling lower back injury, possibly paraplegia.

She returns to her comfortable quarters in the bunkhouse, the sprawling luxury apartment complex where employees of Cretaceous World are entitled to live rent-free. She's a security guard at the dinosaur park and so has the right to a place here. She shares her spacious apartment with her spouse, a long-haul truck driver named Sarah. Sarah doesn't work for CW herself but is entitled to live in the bunkhouse because of her marriage to Larissa. Sarah is gone on a Coast-to-Coast run out to New Jersey and back and won't be home for a couple weeks.

Larissa hurries through a dinner of vegetables and rice with green tea. Then she gets ready to go out. She takes off her gi and showers. Some purists might fault her for wearing her gi outside the dojo, but she doesn't care about fussy rules like that. She's about getting the job done, not following all the etiquette down to the last little detail. She puts on African-themed clothing and looks at herself in the mirror. She sees a tall Black woman with a big Afro looking back at her. She smiles, then remembers what she has to do tonight. The smile vanishes.

She goes to her car in the adjoining parking structure. As the silent vehicle comes to the stop sign where it will turn left to go down the hill, she looks right and sees the palatial residence up on the hillside. It's gleaming white in the moonlight. She imagines it's the castle where the daimyo lives. She likes to imagine she's a samurai in service to the lord of Cretaceous World.

She drives through the dark, aware that there are dinosaurs around her. She feels the way time connects over millions and millions of years here in this unique spot in space and temporality. Even climate change loops back a hundred million years here to a period when the average temperature was much higher than it was a century ago.

She drives until Cretaceous World has been left behind. She's now moving through the late hours of Labor Day in 2117. She's beyond the borders of the dinosaur park. Here global warming isn't just a help to imagining what it was like during the Cretaceous and late Jurassic. Climate change has disrupted the global economy. Billions of human lives are falling apart. Big problems ensue: marital problems, economic problems, problems with disordered thinking, political problems, and just plain death. Hundreds of millions have died around the planet as a result of drought, flood, war, and plague. Larissa can't fix all that, of course. What she's dedicated to doing is protecting the idyllic realm of Cretaceous World from outside threats.

Larissa is proactive. She knows the police won't act until someone has actually committed a crime. A man in the Albina District of Portland has been sending deranged threats to Cretaceous World, and Larissa has been made aware of them through her job in the security force. The man has been traced to an address on Humboldt Street not far from where she grew up. She's going to knock on his front door and try to talk with him. At the very least, she'll size this guy up and assess the threat level he poses.

There've been several nut-jobs she's had to deal with this year, all of them male and all of them inside the dinosaur park. This is the first time in a long while she's had to leave the park to do her job.

There was the bomber in the T-rex station last February. That was a scary one. The guy reasoned that these dinosaurs aren't natural, are artificial, and so don't have a place in the current ecosystem. Somehow he leapt from that logic to the conclusion that he should bomb Cretaceous World as a gesture of protest. He brought an improvised explosive device into the park's train system concealed in his backpack. Something about him had made Larissa suspicious. She followed him to the T-rex station, and when she saw him set the backpack down and walk away, she moved in to arrest him. He didn't surrender quietly. He reached out to push her away, and she did katatori nikkyo on him, creating an excruciating pain in his wrist that drove him down to his knees and kept him there while she hooked him up with the handcuffs. She called for the paddy wagon and had him carted off to the jail just down the road in Dewberry. The park actually does have a bomb expert, and he raced to the scene and used a robot to put the backpack in a thick steel box. The T-rex station had been evacuated, of course. The bomb was taken to a solitary location and blown up inside the steel box using a stick of dynamite. The steel box was ruined along with the exploding backpack, but that was no big deal. The park had plenty of steel boxes on hand.

Then there was the minor incident that happened a couple weeks ago. No audio is allowed in the park. Ear buds and headphones only. One young man wanted to play his music out loud for everyone to hear. Larissa warned him, but he didn't want to be governed by park rules. So after warning him a second time, she escalated to taking away his music-maker. When he tussled with her, she immobilized him using sankyo. He couldn't move without feeling his elbow was coming apart, which made it easy to put the cuffs on him. The wagon showed up, and she shipped him off to the Dewberry jail on charges of resisting arrest.

There was even an assault by an old man last May. Always the men! So far she hasn't needed to use aikido against a single woman in all her years as a security guard at Cretaceous World. The old fellow had a walking stick and tried to poke Larissa in the face when she told him to stop trying to poke a teenager who was annoying him. She used shihonage, the four-directions throw, to put the old gent on the floor and confiscate his stick. Him she just booted out of the park. Respect for seniors kept her from tossing him in jail.

The car continues silently through the night. Traffic is light, so the night stays dark. Larissa's thoughts turn to Sarah. She pictures her pale skin and her short blond hair. She wants to touch them right now. She reaches out and taps Sarah's number on the speed dial of the car phone. She hears the call trying to raise a response on the phone in Sarah's truck wherever it is at this moment.

These words from a Japanese novel she's reading appear and linger in her mind:

"Like dry ground welcoming the rain, she lets the solitude, silence, and loneliness soak in."

Sarah's honeyed voice comes over the continent and out of the car phone, "Hello. This is Sarah."

Larissa brightens and says, "Hello, my love."

Sarah's voice brightens too, "I'm so glad you called. I'm in a huge truck stop in Iowa surrounded by lonely male drivers who all seem to think I'm the answer to their prayers."

Larissa laughs, "Or to their fantasies anyway. I'm guessing those boys don't do a lot of praying."

Sarah says, "I don't know about that. Out here, they probably do. It's different. I haven't gone Coast to Coast in a long while. I used to do this a lot when I was driving for Swift. Since I became an owner-operator, I've been sticking closer to home."

Larissa says, "I know."

Sarah says, "Yeah, you do. I'm kind of talking to myself, I guess. One of the hazards of long haul."

They're silent for a few moments.

Sarah says, "Twenty tons of dinosaur T-shirts from a small warehouse in Portland to a big warehouse in New Jersey. It's an easy run, really. Good weather. Just rolling along the Interstate."

Larissa says, "I miss you, honey."

Sarah says, "Me too."

Larissa says, "I can't wait for you to get back home."

Sarah says, "Yeah, me either."

They're silent again. Their intimacy is as tangible as an embrace.

Sarah asks, "So what are you doing tonight?"

Larissa lies, "Oh, just missing you. I'll probably go to bed early."

She doesn't want Sarah to know that she's driving to Portland to confront a man who's been sending threats to Cretaceous World. She doesn't want her to worry. She also doesn't want her to know anything about it. If things go wrong, she doesn't want Sarah to become a witness in some kind of investigation that might follow. You never know. If Sarah were paying attention, she could tell that the call was coming from the car phone. She's not though. Even if she did notice, Larissa could just say she's driving down to the supermarket in Dewberry for groceries.

Larissa asks, "You know what I've been thinking about tonight?"

Sarah asks, "What have you been thinking about tonight?"

Larissa says, "You know. Our raising a baby together."

Sarah just says, "Yeah, I know."

They've been over this many times before. They've talked about adopting. They've talked about one or the other of the two of them using sperm from a donor. They've talked about their baby looking African-American or Scots-Irish and how they'd feel about either outcome. They've talked about adopting an Asian child or Latin American or American Indian. They've talked about the excellent child care Cretaceous World offers free for children of employees. They've talked about the superb private school, the Winston Academy, that provides a world-class K-12 education free of charge for kids of park employees. They've talked about the full scholarship that the park gives to all children of employees who are admitted to any university or college in the world. They've talked about it all. They haven't decided not to do it, whichever version of it it is. They just haven't decided to do it either.

They talk a little longer and then hang up.

Larissa puts on a medley of mid-twentieth-century jazz in the car's sound system. Charlie Parker, Dizzy Gillespie, John Coltrane, Miles Davis: she loves the inventive power of this music. She's proud of it too. It's all men though, and that bothers her a little. Not enough to get in the way of her pleasure. The truth of her visceral response to this music is irresistible.

She thinks of the lights of the truck stop where Sarah is parked right now. She thinks they'd seem beautiful if she could see them. She makes her way through the Terwilliger curves south of Portland and approaches the downtown. From the Interstate east of the river, the lights of the tall buildings are lovely. She passes them and exits the freeway in North Portland. She makes her way to the neighborhood she knows so well, the one where she grew up.

It's around midnight when she pulls up in front of the house on Humboldt Street and parks. This is still a quiet neighborhood, just as it was when she lived here. Some of the houses are remodeled, fancier now. Some new townhouses have appeared. She imagines the property values have gone up a lot.

She knows some things about the man who lives in this house. He has a police record, and since she's a security guard at Cretaceous World, she has full access to the police database that keeps track of these things. The owner of the dinosaur park that employs her is very rich and very influential, and he has made sure that his park's security force knows everything the police know about people who've run afoul of the law.

She knows that the man who lives here has served in the Army and has seen combat in Pakistan and North Korea. She knows he's White and divorced. She knows there are many complaints against him from his neighbors. She knows he killed a man on his front porch last year but was found innocent by a jury of his peers because they believed he was acting in self-defense.

She readies herself to live or die. She concentrates on the Ki principles: she finds the one-point in her lower abdomen; she relaxes her muscles completely; she brings her weight underside; she extends Ki out her arms and legs and head and spherically out from her hara.

She walks up the concrete steps to the wide covered porch. She knocks on the door and waits. After a short while, she knocks again and waits. She sees a light go on upstairs. She waits. Then she pounds on the door loud and long. She hears footsteps coming down the stairs. She waits.

She knows it's late. She knows it's odd to be pounding on the front door of a house in a quiet neighborhood at this hour. She doesn't care. She wants to catch this guy off guard. She wants to find out what to expect from him before he possibly brings it to the park. An ounce of prevention.

The porchlight goes on. The door opens. A man steps forward holding a pistol in his right hand. He looks like the mugshot she has seen in the police database.

Larissa had been going to ask him if he was Ronald Johnson when he opened the door. Now that question is moot. He's someone who's pointing a gun directly at her. That's all the ID she needs now.

Without hesitation, she rotates slightly offline so a bullet will just barely miss her. As good as a mile. Simultaneously with the small rotation, she uses Ki to raise her left arm in a very quick motion. Her left hand softly grabs the back of the gun-hand and sticks to it with adhesive Ki as she blends with the natural forward motion of the man's right arm. The arm is drawn forward a foot or so as she brings her right hand up onto the gun's barrel. She rotates her body back the other direction, extending Ki out her right arm and naturally bending the direction of the gun back towards the attacker. The gun comes loose from the man's hand, and she pulls the trigger. Aikido is life or death. The bullet destroys his heart instantly, shutting off blood to the brain. A moment later, he loses consciousness. He's dead before he hits the ground.

With her left hand, Larissa pulls a handkerchief out of her jacket pocket and uses it to take the gun out of her right hand. Then she uses a corner of the handkerchief to wipe her fingerprint off the trigger. She puts the gun back into the hand of the dead man and presses his trigger-finger against the trigger lightly but firmly. Using her foot, she nudges the weapon out of his hand and leaves it a short distance away.

She feels his neck at the spot where the big artery runs through. As expected, she feels no hint of a pulse.

She looks around at the neighborhood. No lights have come on in nearby houses so far as she can tell. A single loud sound hasn't been enough to disturb the tranquility of this place. That's about to change.

Or will it?

She stops and thinks. What if she just leaves now? Why open a can of worms? Quietly fleeing the scene might work out. It might not though, and Larissa just couldn't face that. She doesn't want to live with that hanging over her head. Other people at Cretaceous World know about this guy and his threats and know she knew about him. Her neighbors at the bunkhouse might have noticed she was gone during the time the guy died. Her phone records could be checked and reveal that she called Sarah from the car phone around that time. She has no alibi for the time of the murder. And so on. It would all unravel once it got started. Better to be a heroic security guard who has been attacked while working to protect the park.

She pulls out her phone and dials 911. After three rings, an operator asks her the nature of her emergency.

Larissa says, "A man's been shot. I think he's dead."

The die is cast. Now it begins. The gears of the machine begin to turn.

Soon she hears the two sirens, the one of the emergency vehicle and the other of the police car, both approaching the peace and quiet of Humboldt Street.

She looks up and sees the moon shining above the water tower. She looks over at the school on the corner where she went when she was a little girl.

The emergency vehicle arrives first. The uniformed man and woman take a look at the body and confirm that the man is dead.

The police arrive at this point and declare that it's a crime scene so no one touch anything until they say it's okay.

Larissa tells one of the cops, the big guy, her sad but heroic story.

He summarizes, "So you're unarmed, and your life was in danger."

She nods.

He says, "I need to pat you down for weapons."

He looks a little embarrassed.

She suppresses a smile and says sure.

He summarizes further, "So you're a security guard. Were you ever a cop? Just curious."

She shakes her head no.

He hands her back her ID and says, "It looks like a clear case of life or death for you. You can go now, but you may need to answer some more questions down the road a little. Keep yourself available to talk with us. Don't become hard to find all of a sudden."

She agrees and leaves. As she drives back south along the Interstate beside the river, she admires the charming lights of downtown Portland.

On the way home, she decides to lead the class at the dojo in munetsuki kotegaeshi this evening, the technique she'd just employed to defeat a man with a gun. Trust your aikido always. Accept the outcome as your destiny. That's what she will tell her students in the pure space and time of the dojo.

DRUMS

I ask Bud, "So what do you think: are you going to apply for Lana's old job?"

He laughs, "Me? Nah, too much hassle. I like doing what I'm doing now. I'm not looking for a change."

I say, "More money?"

He says, "Got what I need already. I'm happy as a clam."

We provide so well for our employees here at Cretaceous World that ambition seldom comes from external motivations. It has to come from within.

Bud climbs up into the cab of the crane and fires up the large, powerful electric engine. He raises the load of food for the Pachycephalosaurs until it's thirty feet off the ground, well above the high wall. He expertly rotates the load out over the pen and drops the ton of food onto the ground.

Araucarian cones, cycad leaves, ferns, mushrooms, and Gingko cherries: the Pachycephalosaurs have a savory diet. They also have a keen sense of smell. Even though the pen is as big as the one for the Triceratops, ten miles by seven miles, it doesn't take them long to come running out of the riparian woods and across the field to the piles of food.

I have a clear view of them from my vantage point on the side of the small hill next to the crane. They're good runners, bipedal, powerful hind legs, fifteen feet long, a thousand pounds heavy, petite and nimble for our array of dinosaurs.

Bud knows what he's doing. He's created two piles of food fifty feet apart. This is because the Pachycephalosaurs are built for butting. Head-butting. They have a rounded bony layer ten inches thick on top of their heads. They have short necks with sturdy neck-bones plus strong neck muscles, tough backbones, and mighty thighs. They're inclined to deliver terrible blows with the bony dome atop their skulls. They did this 65 to 68 million years ago in order to bash rivals and predators. There are no predators in their pen, of course, and there's only one male and one female, which keeps the rivalry to a minimum. Still, it's wise to make it possible for them to eat off separate piles so they're less likely to clash about food. They really are quite pugnacious by temperament, very quick to anger.

They have peglike teeth at the front of their mouths and triangular crowns at the rear. They have big cheeks so they can chop up the rough food thoroughly before swallowing it and sending it down to their big bellies for gut processing. I love the way their long tails stretch out behind them as they eat. The tails sway slightly as if in a gentle breeze. They're bent over, of course, and their small arms, each with five clawed fingers, help guide the food into their mouths. The four long toes on their sturdy feet keep them stable yet ready to flee if a T-rex comes plodding up, which it won't here at our nice, safe amusement park.

I want to hear Becky laughing, "What do you think this is: an amusement park?"

I suddenly feel very angry. I want to ram head-first into something. I'd like to be equipped like a Pachycephalosaur and butt old Bud here as hard as I can.

I immediately feel remorse about this. I like Bud. What a monstrous idea.

Bud gets down from the cabin of the crane and walks over to me.

He says, "You know, I miss Lana. I'm real happy for her, but I miss her being around when I'm feeding the dinos."

I smile, "I'll tell her you said hi. I'm going to see her this afternoon."

He says, "Thanks, boss. You're the best."

He climbs into the pickup truck with the park's logo on the side and heads for the next dinosaur pen on his route.

I return to the residence and get ready for the meeting with Lana.

* * * * * * * * * * * *

So I'm in the office showing Lana the ropes. Outside the residence, the afternoon heat of early September 2117 is beating down. In this plush office on the second floor, all is cool and comfortable.

I think, "The point of fate is unknown. The purpose of Nature is unknowable. The meaning of existence may not exist. The world may be absurd. Beauty and truth may be illusions. I'd like to be a Pachycephalosaur right now and ram my head through that wall over there. Every day I'd come here to the office and see the hole I put in the wall. I'd like that."

I ask, "How's it going with the search for your replacement?"

She looks at me carefully.

She asks, "Everything okay? You holding up all right?"

I guess I'm not that hard for her to read. I'm apparently an open book to her.

I say, "I'm missing Becky pretty bad. It just makes me mad sometimes. I'm sorry."

She says, "No need to apologize. It's perfectly understandable. To answer your question: yes, I've narrowed the field down to two candidates I'd like to invite for interviews. Here are their files."

She picks up two manila folders off what is now her desk and hands them to me. I sit down and look through the contents of the folders.

I comment, "One from inside the organization and the other from outside. They both look good. Good work. Sure, bring them in for interviews as soon as possible. I want to move fast on filling your old job."

She smiles, "Will do, boss."

I add, "I saw Bud this morning, by the way. He says hi. He misses you."

She says, "Aw, that's nice of him. Let's see, this morning, that was probably at the Pachycephalosaur pen."

I say, "You're good. Yes, it was."

I notice she's dressing better now that she's working in the residence. Her long blonde hair is brushed and shining. She's wearing perfume and a dress.

She looks into my eyes and smiles, blushing slightly. I really am an open book to her.

She says, "Seriously, let me know if there's anything I can do to help you, you know, with what you were talking about, missing Becky, feeling angry. Anything."

"That's generous of you, but I'm fine. Really. Let's go over how you read the weekly financial statements sent by central accounting down at the headquarters. They send them up to us here in a digital spreadsheet every Monday."

She smiles and pays attention to what I'm teaching her about the financial statements and about the many other things that Becky used to do.

I feel Becky beside me looking on. I wish I could hear her voice offering advice and suggestions. As long as her presence is here with me, I don't want to put a hole in the wall anymore. Lana relaxes and doesn't seem worried about me. I stay on topic and make good sense. We make progress.

* * * * * * * * * * * *

There's a Japanese haiku from three centuries ago that applies here. Issa wrote it. It pops into my head as I watch Lana making soup in my kitchen on the private third floor of the residence.

It goes, "Katatsuburi / soro soro nobore / Fuji no yama (The snail keeps climbing / slowly, slowly to the top / of Fuji Mountain)."

I've learned a smattering of many languages, including just enough Japanese to greet our many visitors from Japan, to understand what the aikidoists on our security force are talking about, and to read the wonderful and refreshing haiku of Basho and Issa in transliteration.

Slowly, gradually, patiently, the pretty snail has crept up from the office on the second floor to the restricted third floor where few may enter. In half a year she's done this, so that by March 2118, here she is, making soup for me in my intimate area. Not just any soup, but the soup of life that Becky used to make me.

I think, "I wonder if the snail is wearing panties."

I can tell she's not wearing a bra under her tight, clingy top. It only seems natural to ask whether she's also not wearing panties under that short, loose skirt.

I don't really know how we got here. I remember I grew tired of making the soup of life myself. It's just not the same making it for myself. Lana kept looking at me with her blue eyes and asking if she couldn't help somehow, so I showed her Becky's instructions for making the special soup. There was no stopping Lana then. She insisted and cajoled until finally here she is, carefully combining the ingredients exactly as Becky prescribed.

Lana is standing at the polished pink marble slab on the kitchen island. She's chopping up carrots and celery for the soup. She's got all the ingredients she needs for the soup of life: water, onion, celery, carrots, potatoes, quinoa, lima beans, green beans, shelled edamame, black-eyed peas, green peas, sweet corn, spinach, brown rice. She's got the precise instructions that Becky wrote.

I feel Becky standing beside me now, watching Lana work, looking around with me at the double-wide stainless-steel refrigerator, the rows of handsome maple cabinets, the beautiful red-and-gold tile floor. I feel her ghostly presence pressing up against me. I wish I could put my arm around her while we watch Lana together.

I walk over to the window above the sink. Becky walks with me, presses up against me again when I stop, admires the glorious view with me. A purple sunset is settling in over the panorama of the park spread out before us in sublime magnificence. Beauty may be a delusion, a self-deception, a trick of the human nervous system that has evolved for no particular reason at all. Perhaps many things evolve randomly, for no purpose and with no utility, just because they can. I feel Becky fading from beside me as a consequence of these thoughts. I don't want her to go. A wave of anger washes over me. I'm furious at my weakness, at my inability to keep Becky with me. I'm enraged at the conditions of existence, at life itself, and most of all at death. This enchanting sunset is a trap for lovers, a manipulative lie told by Nature, and worse, a sadistic joke made by the Cosmos.

I can hear my angry heartbeat pounding on my eardrums: thumpa, thumpa, thumpa, turning them into two perfectly synchronized bass drums inside my head.

I'd never want to be involved in a May/December relationship. I'd feel like I was ruining the life of a young woman and setting up a weirdness for a child to be born into. A young man would inevitably show up, someone who could make her happy and give her the kind of life she deserved. Then what? A nasty mess. I'm not the kind of man who could step aside and accept an interloper. I'd understand, but I'd hate him anyway. And if she accepted him, I'd consider it betrayal and hate her too, even though I understood.

There's a story by a writer who lived in this corner of the world more than a century ago. A man is leaving a woman. They each want the baby they've made. Both grab hold of their child and pull, trying to rip it out of the grasp of the other. The baby screams in pain. This is the last thing I'd ever want. I don't think I could bear being responsible for creating that kind of situation for a child. Couples splitting up seldom if ever actually pull their babies apart physically, but psychically they often do exactly that. I'd hate that. I'd loathe being one of those two parents doing that to their innocent child.

These thoughts don't make me less angry.

Things connect in our experience in odd ways. Pachycephalosaurs with big bass drums pounding in my head, the soup of life with the devastation of death and loss.

Thumpa, thumpa, thumpa.

I turn away from the window with its sunset and come up behind Lana, who is still chopping carrots and celery on the pink marble slab of the island.

She glances over her shoulder and says, "You know, these instructions really are wonderful. Becky had a very precise intellect. I hope you don't mind my saying so."

I put my left hand on her shoulder and hold her in place.

I say, "I don't mind. She really did."

I lift up her short skirt with my right hand and find no panties.

I say, "That answers my question. I hope you don't mind."

She doesn't say a thing. She just lowers her head and exhales strongly.

I push her forward with my left hand until she is bent over. I insert the fingers of my right hand into her cunt.

I say, "You see, I'm an odd Pachycephalosaur. I like to head-butt a little differently."

She snorts, "With your other head."

I snort back, "In your lovely butt."

She says breathily, "I've dreamed of doing this with you, just like this."

I observe, "Hence your state of readiness, no bra suggesting no panties."

I feel how wet she's becoming.

I'm still taking the erectile pills every day so I can ejaculate while feeling Becky's presence close by. I unzip.

My anger comes out, and my other head goes in. I pound into her harder and harder.

She mutters, "Yes, O yes, fuck me, fuck me hard."

I grab her beautiful golden hair at the back of her head and yank back on it. I'm now ramming my cock into her wet cunt as hard as I can.

As I come, I have the weird sense that I'm dreaming my son. Not just my child, but my son. Like I'm sleeping and in my dream can create my child and know it's a boy.

I turn Lana around and put her on her knees.

I say, "Open your mouth. Clean me up."

I put my still semi-erect cock in her mouth, and she sucks and licks it clean.

I'm stunned. I'm shocked.

I think, "What have I done? What in the world have I done?"

Then I think, "I've made a grandson for Becky. She'll like that."

I'm not angry at all anymore. I don't exactly know what to do next, but I'm not angry. At least that much is certain.

Lana looks pleased but confused too.

She says, "I didn't see this part written down on the recipe."

She stands up and kisses me on the cheek.

I just don't know what to do.

She says, "Don't worry. Everything is fine. Look, I'm going back to making the soup. It's all okay."

I whisper, "Words fail me."

She starts chopping again, "No need for words. You just make yourself comfortable while I get this soup cooking."

I sit down at the kitchen counter. I look over at the wall beside me. Still no hole in this wall either.

Lana's hair is still disheveled from where I grabbed it and yanked her head back. It's very appealing.

It will take hours for the soup to be ready to eat.

I just don't know what comes next.

I don't leave the room though. It feels wrong to leave Lana alone now.

How did this young, fit woman wind up in my kitchen? She's thirty years old, more or less. I'm about to be seventy. How did this happen?

I watch her hips jiggle as she chops.

An hour passes somehow. Then more time, I don't know how much.

There's more soup than the stockpot can hold, so she's transferring four quarts of soup to a Dutch oven in order to make room for stirring in the spinach.

At some point, the soup is cooking in the two pots.

Lana comes over to where I'm sitting and raises the front of her skirt. Her shaved pussy is right in front of my face.

She asks, "Care for an hors d'oeuvre, sir?"

Those little pills are wondrous things. I find that I'm indeed ready again. Lazarus is risen.

I push her back onto the low countertop and spread her legs open. I unzip and step out of my pants. I slide my miraculous erection into her and ram her over and over with all my might.

This is so much better than knocking a hole in this or that wall.

REAPER

Althea Morgan leaves her luxury hotel and walks west on Main Street toward the Hominid's Delight. There's a fine restaurant in the hotel, but she wants to talk with the locals not tourists. She's come to Dewberry not to visit the amazing dinosaurs of nearby Cretaceous World but to learn more about the shocking murder that happened here a year ago. She hopes it will provide her with the material for her next mystery novel.

She's enjoying this mid-morning in mid-May 2118. The deciduous trees that line Main Street are nearly done leafing out, so she can walk in the beautiful shade. It's a lazy Saturday morning, and traffic is light. The electric vehicles slip silently along, emitting no fumes. The shops she passes are attractive, colorful. The town breathes prosperity. Clearly, the dinosaurs have been good to Dewberry.

Althea is gray, a widow for many years, childless, alone except for the millions of her fans. She's the author of the popular mysteries featuring PI Thomas Reaper. Reaper is a mysterious fellow who solves murders by unconventional means. He's tall, dark, appears and disappears suddenly, an enigma. He's especially good at leading people through what they do know, even though they think they know very little and feel stuck. Reaper guides them to realizations they never would have made on their own.

She reaches the Hominid's Delight and goes in. She's in luck: a table by a big window opens up just as she enters. The waitress shows her to the table and gives her a menu.

Althea say, "Thank you, dear, but I know what I want. I'll have three fried eggs over easy, rye toast with real butter, and black coffee, no sugar, no cream."

The waitress smiles, takes back the menu, and hustles off.

Althea imagines a conversation with the waitress, a thirty-year-old woman who wears no wedding ring.

Althea asks, "Were you here last year when the tourist was murdered?"

The waitress, let's call her Bonnie, replies, "No, but I've heard all about it."

Althea asks for a few details.

Bonnie says, "It was a Russian woman who was killed. She was married to an American, but she was here with another man. So I hear. The killer left a note saying this was just the first of many who were going to die in Dewberry or over at the dinosaur park next door."

Althea thanks Bonnie and thinks, "It's a good start."

Althea looks around and spots the town sheriff and his deputy. They're eating pastries and drinking coffee.

She's amused and thinks, "A continental breakfast for the two lawmen, please."

She imagines asking them about the murdered Russian woman.

The sheriff says, "Very strange. We don't have that sort of thing around here."

The deputy blurts, "She was right here in this restaurant just before she was killed, you know."

The sheriff glares at the deputy, but the deputy just keeps going, "We're watching for a serial killer, you know. There was a note saying this was just the first. Many more to come."

The sheriff interrupts, "You're talking the poor lady's ear off. There's no serial killer. Everything's under control."

The deputy agrees, "That note was just a red herring, I expect. Supposed to throw us off. My money's on the fiancé. She came here with him, but they had a big fight. He was drinking in the hotel bar when she was murdered. She'd stormed out of the hotel and come down here. Witnesses backed up the guy's story. Still, I reckon somehow or other he did it. Or paid someone to do it."

The sheriff insists, "We ruled the fiancé out. No need to imagine things there's no evidence to support."

The deputy adds, "She was flirting with other guys. That's what ticked her fiancé off. She marries an old guy to get into the country and become a citizen. Then she leaves the old gent for a young stud. Why does the fiancé think she's going to stop with him? I figure he decided if he couldn't have her, no one was going to."

The sheriff stands up, "Okay, that's enough. We need to get back to work. Nice talking with you, ma'am. Enjoy your stay in Dewberry. And don't worry: no place is safer than right here."

Althea smiles and says good-bye.

Bonnie brings the eggs, toast, and coffee.

As Althea eats, she overhears two women at the table next to hers. From their conversation she gathers that they live in Dewberry. One sounds like an attorney, and the other sounds like a school teacher.

When Althea has finished her eggs and toast and is enjoying her second cup of rich black coffee, she imagines talking with the two ladies about the murder of the Russian woman.

The attorney, let's call her Brenda, says, "My money's on the husband. That alibi about being home alone in Denver wouldn't hold up very well in court."

The teacher, let's call her Cathy, says, "Can you imagine how he must have felt? His wife just uses him and then tosses him away when she doesn't need him anymore."

Brenda snorts, "You mean like men do to women all the time? Yes, I can imagine. Easily."

Cathy smiles sadly, "It doesn't make it right. He must have been devastated."

Brenda replies, "And furious. His plan to exploit some desperate foreign girl backfired on him. So, of course, he killed her. Or hired a killer to do it. Poor baby. My heart goes out to him."

Cathy scolds softly, "You're terrible. I feel sorry for him. I agree with you though: he probably did it."

Brenda scoffs good-naturedly, "Oh, he did it. I'm sure of it."

Cathy tells Althea, "Don't mind her. She's been this way since her divorce last year."

Althea doesn't tell them she doubts it was the husband, but she does doubt it. They'd just ask her why, and all she'd be able to say is that it would be too obvious, too uninteresting, not a good enough story. She needs something better than that for Reaper to solve.

Althea imagines asking them if there's anyone else here in the Hominid's Delight this morning who might be able to shed some more light on the facts of the terrible crime. They direct her to a couple sitting in a booth against the wall. He's the doctor who first took a look at the body, and she's his wife of thirty years.

Althea imagines talking with the doctor, let's call him Dr. Bob Collins, and his well-dressed wife, let's call her Gloria.

Dr. Collins says, "That was a memorable evening."

Gloria objects, "Please, Bob, not at breakfast."

The doctor looks unhappy. He clearly wants to continue.

Althea explains, "I'm sorry to intrude. It's for the mystery novel I'm writing. Perhaps you've heard of my books, the Thomas Reaper novels? There was a movie out earlier this year based on my book *The Devil in the Details.*"

Gloria's attitude changes abruptly, "Oh, you're that Althea Morgan! Please forgive me. I love your books. And your movies: *A Guess in the Dark* is my favorite. I really thought it should've won an Oscar. What's the title of the book you're working on now?"

Althea confesses, "I don't really have a title yet. The working title is just *The Murder near the Dinosaur Park*, but that obviously will never do. Perhaps something your husband tells me will help me find the right title."

Gloria brightens and looks at Bob.

The doctor says, "The thing that stood out was the way she was killed. Very neatly. No mess, no fury. Not a crime of passion or aggression. Professional and businesslike. Whoever did it was practiced, skillful, like a surgeon, I must say."

Althea says, "My apologies for asking for gory details over brunch, but I really do need to know: how exactly was she killed?"

Dr. Collins explains succinctly, "One bullet to the head, two to the heart. I couldn't tell in which order, but my guess was the head came first, before she even suspected she was in danger. Very quickly: bam, bam-bam. No muss, no fuss. They were small bullets that didn't pass all the way through. One bounced around inside the skull and tore up the brain. The other two shut down the blood-pump instantly. She never knew what hit her."

Althea thinks, "Yes, definitely a professional hit."

She says, "Thank you so much for your time. Again, I apologize for intruding."

They insist it's no problem at all. Gloria persuades Althea to let her take a selfie of their three heads together. The Collins look radiantly pleased as Althea returns to her table.

Bonnie arrives with a coffee refill and mentions that the bartender at the hotel where the Russian woman stormed out had himself disappeared that same night.

Bonnie says, "A friend of mine, Betty, actually went out with the guy. He was Russian too. Quite the good-looker."

Althea imagines asking how she can talk with Betty.

Bonnie says, "No problem. She's sitting right over there. She's on break. She's a waitress here too."

Betty tells Althea, "I was stuck on the guy. I thought we had something good going. Then he just vanished into thin air. He didn't leave a trace."

Althea asks, "Did you tell the police about this?"

Betty replies, "Well, I told the sheriff, but he didn't seem to think it was any big thing."

Althea persists, "But being Russian too and disappearing on the night of the murder: all that didn't raise any red flags?"

Betty is puzzled, "No. What red flags? Red flags about what?"

Althea says, "Oh, nothing. It's nothing at all. Never mind. Can you think of anything else that was strange about his disappearance, anything at all?"

Betty thinks a minute and says, "Well, my friend Beverly is a cocktail waitress at the same bar where Konstantin worked. That's his name: Konstantin. Sexy name, isn't it? It gets me a little excited just saying it again. Anyway, Beverly said she was working the night he disappeared. She saw the Russian woman, Vera was her name apparently, get into a big fight with her fiancé and blow out of the place. Then she saw my beautiful Konstantin rush out right after that."

Althea says, "Never to be seen again, as they say."

Betty nods sadly.

Althea thanks her and returns to her own table by the big window.

Bonnie shows up, coffee pot in hand, and Althea accepts her fourth cup of strong black coffee.

Althea thinks, "Clearly the bartender did it. The murderous charmer. He did his job. The husband got his revenge. Jezebel was punished brutally, permanently. All I need now are the gritty details."

* * * * * * * * * * * *

She goes over to the dinosaur park that afternoon and gathers some picturesque odds and ends. They'll be especially good for the movie.

She thinks, "People always love dinosaurs. Dinosaurs and Reaper: can't miss with that combo."

Althea begins to detect the ethereal fragrance of approaching success.

Standing in the fossil museum at Cretaceous World, she thinks,

"*Murder for the Ages.*"

She has her title.

She looks around at all the bones of all the amazing creatures from so many millions of years ago. She becomes determined to use all this. She's resolute. She must include these wonderful things in a lavish context for Thomas Reaper's next triumph as the supreme supersleuth of the 22nd century.

REEDS

You know, sitting here at the Hadrosaur pen, I really regret that our dinosaurs can't lay eggs that will hatch.

I say Hadrosaur, but I mean specifically our two Edmontosaurs. These were the most abundant herbivorous dinosaurs at the end of the Cretaceous. When the asteroid six miles wide struck the Earth some sixty-five million years ago, it killed a very large number of Edmontosaurs, each of them similar to our pair here at Cretaceous World.

One big difference is that none of our dinosaurs can beget offspring. Our genetic engineers purposely made them unable to reproduce. I wish Ned and Nora here, our nicknames for these two, could create eggs that would be laid in nests in the ground to hatch and bring forth progeny. I wish these amazing animals could roam the land again in vast herds.

Look at them down there in the cool morning. Aren't they wonderful?

They're warm-blooded, so we can feed them early before the brutal heat of late summer 2118 builds and spreads. They used to migrate seasonally from the Arctic Circle to what is now southern Alberta and back. They're vigorous at relatively cool temperatures.

Unlike their aggressive Ornithischian relatives the Pachycephalosaurs who have to be fed in separate food-piles lest they head-butt each other, the Hadrosaurs are quite gregarious and enjoy each other's company. They'll happily graze right beside each other at one big pile of vegetation.

When we dumped the several tons of nourishment into their pen this morning, they came splashing eagerly across the mud and reeds of the marsh. Now they're quite pleased to be filling their bellies side by side.

Listen, Ned raises his long flat head and uses the skin flaps around his nostrils to bellow. It sounds a lot like a baritone sax, doesn't it?

Sit beside me here on this hillside in the shade and watch them eating. Look at their broad, edentulous beaks. Aren't they just like ducks' bills? Marvelous, aren't they?

They have no teeth at the front of their long mouths. They scoop up rough vegetation with their duck-bills and chop it up with the hundreds of teeth in the dental batteries at the rear of their mouths. Their cheeks keep the food in their mouths while they chew it.

Nora raises her head and bellows in answer to Ned. Don't you love it? It's just like another baritone saxophone responding to the first. It's fantastic. Imagine a whole herd of them. Imagine little juveniles coming through the reeds and mud and feeding with their parents. Such a beautiful dream. I wish it were so. I wish I could see that.

Hadrosaur in Greek means a lizard that's stout, bulky, thick. They do have big bellies. They don't have grinding teeth and don't have gizzards full of rocks, so they need massive digestive equipment to process the very rough, fibrous food they scoop up, chop up, and swallow.

They always look like they're pregnant, both female and male, so it's weird to see them running at their top speed of thirty miles per hour, or even just loping along at their cruising speed of fifteen miles per hour.

They're forty feet long and nine thousand pounds with the aforementioned broad abdomens, yet they run like deer, like gazelles, with the exception that they often pick up their long front limbs and become bipedal when they're dashing merrily about in their enormous pen, ten miles by seven.

They're built to graze on the low-growing angiosperms that regenerate very quickly. Although they can rise up on their hind legs to reach the leaves in the trees, they're mainly designed to go low easily. Their spine slopes downward gracefully from their shoulders into their neck which continues naturally toward the ground, so they're able to keep their mouth close to low vegetation indefinitely and with little effort.

Look at them down there in the morning coolness. They're truly fabulous, aren't they?

* * * * * * * * * * * *

Lana is six months pregnant. Her belly now reminds me of Ned's and Nora's this morning at the Hadrosaur pen. It's September 25, 2118. Her tummy bulge has grown big enough that it's hard for her to bend very far forward. I've started to help her with certain tasks that have become difficult or impossible for her to do herself.

Tonight, for instance, we're lying naked on the vast bed in the master bedroom on the third floor of the residence, and I'm shaving her pubic hair with a razor. I kind of like doing this. It definitely beats clipping her toenails and cleaning out the dainty goo from under them. She's just stepped out of the shower, so the hairs are soft and don't need shaving cream.

When I've finished shaving her mons smooth, I pull back her labia with my thumbs and gently lick her clitoris. It's clean and tastes nice and tangy. I can feel it growing firmer against my tongue. She develops a little erection, which I continue to stroke with my tongue. After some very agreeable minutes, she shudders and gasps, and I know by her trembling that she's coming. When she's relaxed again, I stop.

She says, "That's what I like about you old guys: you know how to treat a woman right."

I ask, "Having sex with a lot of old guys, are we?"

She laughs, "Not since I moved up here to the big house on the hill."

She's gone from the bunkhouse to the residence to the master quarters. She now lives with the king at the top of the palace overlooking the realm. I sometimes wonder if I'd appeal to her at all if I weren't the lord of the manor. It's a childish question, and I don't voice it. I do wonder though.

She pats her belly and asks, "So when are you going to make an honest woman of me, sir?"

I answer with a question, "Is that a proposal?"

She smiles, "Sure, why not?"

She pulls her knees up high and spreads her legs wide, tilting her head a wee bit to the side and continuing with the alluring little smile.

She's grown her wavy blond hair out longer since she moved up here, and it's hanging down now onto her left breast.

I say, "Another thing about old men is they don't always think with their penis."

She winks, "You don't say."

Her shapely legs remain spread in wide-open invitation.

I continue, "I really shouldn't. It's unwise."

She says, "How so? Enlighten me, master."

I think, "Don't talk, Ted. Don't spoil things. That's Becky's grandchild in her belly. Don't alienate the mother."

Then I think, "That makes me Becky's husband and her son, in effect."

I do talk though.

I say, "Here's the thing, ... "

She guesses, "It's you, not me."

I confirm, "Yeah, in a way."

She smirks and shakes her head.

I say, "Part of my problem is I don't want to move on from Becky's death. I don't want to leave her behind. I want to be a widower who continues to live with her vivid memory for the rest of life."

She nods, "I know. I understand."

I say, "But equally important to me, I don't want to create a crazy situation for our child, yours and mine."

She pats her belly, "It's a little late for that now."

I say, "I don't want our child to feel torn between loyalties to you and to me. I want to be practical for the sake of the child."

I pause.

She says, "Go on. I'm listening."

I say, "What I think will work is if Becky and I are the grandparents. Grandma and grandpa, that's us. You're mama."

She asks, "And who will we say is papa?"

I say, "That's the big question. We need to create an answer for that inevitable question. We've got some time before the child can speak or remember later what happens now. While the little brain is growing and developing greater cognitive abilities, we'll see if we can find someone to be papa. I'll work with you on this. I have some ideas. I'm thinking I'll do a national search for a protégé, a person I can train to replace me as head of this whole operation here at Cretaceous World. It's a lifelong commitment, and it will be appropriate and necessary to inquire into personal details that are not proper in most job interviews. Marital status, personal relationships, such things will be relevant when searching for someone to dedicate the rest of his life to the continued well-being of our unique enterprise here at the park. You'll go through the applications and take part in the interviews. We'll pick out someone you like. It'll be like a matchmaking service in the guise of filling a key position at the top of the organizational chart. I'm sure I can sell Randy Winston on this, the need for me to develop someone to take over for me when I'm done. He was explicit with me when he told me to find a replacement for Becky's role in the organization. We're lucky that the owner is such a clear-sighted person and so reasonable. We won't tell him about the need for you and me to find a daddy for our child, of course."

She grunts, "Huh. That's quite an idea you've got there, professor."

I say, "I'll be there for you. I'll always be there. I want to be a daily part of our child's life. I'll take care of you both. You'll never want for anything."

She's been looking at me directly with her big blue eyes. Now she turns them aside and looks away from me.

She says softly, "I love you."

It hurts me, but I know what I have to say.

I think, "Becky, forgive me, I'll always love you only."

I say, "I love you too. And I love our child."

I'm glad Lana's gaze was averted so she couldn't see my momentary hesitation, couldn't observe the conflict on my face for a split-second.

I think, "I wish we were young again, Becky. I envy this young woman. She's the mother of your grandchild. I'll make sure mother and child have a good life."

I roll Lana on her side and spoon her.

I think, "I've got to find a young man to do this for her. This is nice, and I'll miss it. There's no future in it though, not the future I want anyway. It's all going to work out fine. I'll make it work out just fine."

* * * * * * * * * * * *

Around one a.m. on Christmas morning, Anno Domini 2118, I'm up in the tower on the fourth floor of the residence. As is my custom on this mythic holiday, I'm reading the Nativity section in the Gospel of Luke in Koinē Greek.

This year, the lines that are especially meaningful to me are these:

1:57-58 - Τῇ δὲ Ἐλεισάβετ ἐπλήσθη ὁ χρόνος τοῦ τεκεῖν αὐτήν, καὶ ἐγέννησεν υἱόν. καὶ ἤκουσαν οἱ περίοικοι καὶ οἱ συγγενεῖς αὐτῆς ὅτι ἐμεγάλυνεν Κύριος τὸ ἔλεος αὐτοῦ μετ' αὐτῆς, καὶ συνέχαιρον αὐτῇ.

"To Elizabeth indeed the time was fulfilled for her to give birth; and her neighbors and relatives heard that the Lord had magnified his mercy to her, and they rejoiced with her."

I'm playing a woodwind quintet on the tower's sound system. The five reed instruments are playing classic Christmas songs without the words. The baritone saxophone makes me think of the Edmontosaurs communicating their happiness with each other.

Directly below me in the master bedroom on the third floor, Lana and little Fred, who is one week old now, are sleeping peacefully. Or maybe Fred woke up and is at this moment nursing contentedly at his mama's bountiful bosom.

At the hospital in Eugene, I didn't try to hide the fact that I was the baby's dad, so I was allowed in the delivery room. It was a relatively easy delivery, only about five hours from onset of labor to baby Fred's popping out. Laura only had an hour at most of really intense pain.

Fred's head was nice and round, not mashed and bruised-looking as happens sometimes with the long deliveries where the soft noggin is lodged in the narrow passageway for a long time. He was beautiful right from the start.

He's a perfect baby. He's definitely got his mom's good looks. I love him so much.

The woodwinds are playing "Silent Night".

I sing, "Holy infant so tender and mild, sleep in heavenly peace. Sleep in heavenly peace."

I repeat the words from Luke: "And her neighbors and relatives heard that the Lord had magnified his mercy to her, and they rejoiced with her."

That's the problem with my idea of finding a young papa for Fred and being good old grandpa myself. Everyone in our little community of Cretaceous World and the neighboring Dewberry area are beaming joyfully at us wherever we go and congratulating us as the parents. My idea will never work. No one around here is going to believe I'm the grandfather. They'll certainly never buy it that someone I bring in a year or so later is the father, or my son; and they know Lana's not my daughter. It's an absurd plan.

I think Lana realized all this right away. She just gave me the time to figure it out for myself.

Not that I actually have it figured out. What I've just figured out really is that I don't have this situation figured out. What I've just realized is the full difficulty of the dilemma I face.

We can't create an environment of lies for Fred to grow up in, lies that no one is going to believe, no one who lives around here anyway.

Everyone here is going to know that I'm Fred's father. It's a small community. Secrets are hard to keep, even for us up here in the palatial residence. Maybe especially for us, since everyone's attention is focused on our doings.

Yet I can't agree to remarry. I want to live with Becky's unfading memory for the rest of my life. I want to remain married to my beloved Becky until I die. I want to feel her presence, to present Fred to her as our grandson, to be grandpa and grandma with her, even though she's no longer counted among the living.

These two things contradict, yet the former is unavoidable while the latter I must do. It's a true dilemma. I don't know exactly how I'll work it out. I'm sure I'll be doing a good bit of fumbling around, gradually finding my way.

The five reed instruments are now playing "Hark the Herald Angels Sing."

I sing, "Glory to the newborn king!"

I get up from the recliner sofa at the center of the room's circle and walk over to where the windows overlook Cretaceous World.

It's a clear night, moonless and dark.

I see the lights of the park headquarters and physical plant, of the employee bunkhouse further down, and of the fossil museum, the park restaurant, the gift shop, the multistory parking garage, and the main subway station by the entry portal to our realm here.

All of this was our child, Becky's and mine. We conceived and oversaw the design and construction of this place and everything in it. It was our baby.

Someone once explained to me the meaning of the Russian word остранение, "making it strange." A work of art can make the world new again, the way a very young child sees it, free of preconceptions and habitual patterns of perception, full of the original wonder and mystery of existence. This park does that: we invite people in to see imitations of beings from 65 to 150 million years ago and to imagine this great stream of time that is the history of life on Earth, this immense and ceaseless flow that we're part of, each one of us with every breath we take.

Suddenly I see something very strange. On the ledge outside the window, a raven sits. It has one white feather on its shoulder but otherwise is shiny black.

I say, "Respite and nepenthe from the memories of Lenore."

Poe is a favorite of mine, a most scientific tale-teller who predicted the concept of the Big Bang.

Looking at this charismatic bird, I have the weird sensation, the bizarre conviction really, that this mysterious little avian dinosaur is somehow connected to Becky. In fact, I have the crazy notion that it actually is Becky somehow. I'm a scientist, but I still respect what I can't explain.

I think, "Nevermore."

One thing I know for sure, I'm never leaving Becky behind so long as I live. I won't stop hoping to rejoin her after I die.

ORBIT

Roger Bridges, the famed astronaut, the man who saved the Earth from that giant asteroid, that cosmic chunk of rock that was as big as the one that hit Chicxulub some 65 million years ago and subsequently destroyed all the non-avian dinosaurs, this very Roger Bridges, the renowned hero, rings the doorbell at the palatial residence on the prominence overlooking Cretaceous World.

Chandler answers the door and says, "Yes, sir."

Roger identifies himself and his reason for being there.

Chandler says, "Welcome, sir. Dr. Beebe is expecting you. Please, come in."

Roger enters the magnificent domicile and follows Chandler up the giant spiral staircase to the conference room on the second floor.

The director of Cretaceous World, Ted Beebe, and the operations manager, Lana Gable, are waiting for Roger. They stand and greet him warmly. Ted introduces him to Lana. They all sit down together at the big table in front of the windows.

Ted asks Roger, "Can we get you anything, some tea or coffee?"

Roger chooses coffee with cream and honey.

Ted says to Chandler, "Coffee with cream and honey for our guest, and tea with lemon for the two of us."

Chandler goes off to carry out the order.

Roger looks out the wall of windows at the panoramic view of the central area of the park, and he comments, "Quite the view."

Ted and Lana smile politely.

Ted says, "I've come to take it for granted after all these years."

They chat a bit, and Chandler soon arrives with the coffee and tea.

Ted asks, "How can we help you to accomplish your goals for your visit here? We've read your letter. We want to do everything we can to make this a useful and enjoyable trip for you."

Roger says, "I appreciate that. I'm especially interested in the dinosaur species that were living when the asteroid smacked into the planet."

Lana reports, "Five of our nine species were there at the sudden end of the Cretaceous: T-rex; the Pachycephalosaur; the Hadrosaur, specifically the Edmontosaur; the Ankylosaur; and the Triceratops."

Ted adds, "I'll be happy to take you with me to see them at feeding time. It's the best way. Much less waiting before they show up. General tourists don't have access to the feeding areas. Security issues, you know. Plus liability and all that. How long will you be staying here in the area?"

Roger replies, "Three weeks. I'm staying at the Embassy Suites in Dewberry. I'd love to see the dinosaurs at feeding time. That's very kind of you."

They all smile. They all feel this meeting is going well.

It's April 2119, over thirty years after those most glorious hours when Roger so heroically diverted the asteroid that was coming to do something devastatingly similar to what the other asteroid had done 65 million years earlier.

Ted says, "So, here we three sit today, pleasantly sipping our tea and coffee, because a few decades ago you succeeded in preventing a global catastrophe."

Roger smiles and nods blandly.

He's extremely fit, even in old age, and has a certain quiet charisma.

Lana says, "You're the greatest hero in human history. It's no exaggeration at all to say that."

Roger smiles and nods again.

Ted says, "I'd really like to hear the details."

Lana adds, "Yes, begin at the beginning. How did you become an astronaut?"

Roger seems detached. He's long since ceased to enjoy the adulation of admirers. He understands it though and accepts it.

He says succinctly, "I went to the Air Force Academy, and after graduation, I became a jet fighter pilot. When I left the service, I became a test pilot. Then I applied to become an astronaut, and they let me in. I was living on the space station orbiting the Earth when the call came over the radio."

Roger pauses, and Lana and Ted wait.

Roger continues, "They said, you know, we have a problem. They told us about the asteroid. It fell to me to take the small maneuverable vehicle and head out into space. I fired a series of electron-powered

guided missiles that were targeted to hit the same spot on the side of
the asteroid at five-minute intervals. Each missile was tipped with plas-
tic explosive and a small container of oxygen that allowed the explosion
to occur. Little by little, the sequence of strong explosions altered the
course of the gigantic rock so that it missed the Earth by almost a hundred thousand miles."

Lana and Ted are staring. They don't appear to know what to say.
They're looking at the man who saved everything they've ever cared
about.

Roger is used to this. He's been the world's biggest celebrity for so
long that it seems normal to him now.

He says, "It was the high point of my life, the biggest thrill. Nothing has ever matched it since. Nothing ever could or ever will. In a
way, my life was over at that very moment. It's all been looking back-
ward ever since then. Not that I'm complaining. I've been extremely
fortunate. It's just the way it is."

* * * * * * * * * * * *

Roger and Ted are sitting on a hillside together the next morning. They're watching Dorothy the T-rex eat her breakfast. Ted has
explained that the male T-rex must be fed miles away on the other
side of the huge pen because the female is bigger and will likely kill or
maim the male if he comes near her food. The only exception is when
the female wants sex and invites the male in. Ted mentions that everyone who works at Cretaceous World calls the male T-rex Roger, which
amuses Roger the astronaut greatly.

Ted gets Roger talking about his life again.

Roger says, "As I told you yesterday, my life sort of ended when
I managed to change the course of that asteroid. No thrill has ever
come close to that one. After I returned to Earth, I wasn't ready for
being a celebrity. It went to my head in a big way. Money just fell out
of the sky: endorsements, commercials, speaking fees, mountains of
cash piled up faster than I could count it. My behavior deteriorated.
My marriage fell apart. My wife and I'd already grown apart during
the year I was away on the space station. After our divorce, she didn't
take long to find a new husband and start a family. I was glad she and
I hadn't done that, start a family. Kids would've gotten in the way of
my near total self-absorption. I carried on like that, indulging myself

in every possible way, until I just got tired of it. Now I'm not very interested in ordinary life. It takes something like these dinosaurs you've got here to get through to me these days."

Ted doesn't know what to say. He feels like he's listening to someone who's basically talking to himself.

The two men sit in silence. The birds sing, the warm breeze rustles the branches, the T-rex eats greedily.

Ted finally ventures to ask, "So what's the point of it all? You saved life on Earth: what's it all about? What's it for?"

Roger says, "Being able to save it all didn't automatically make me wise. Best I can tell, life exists for its own sake. The purpose of life is just staying alive."

Ted persists, "Truth, beauty, justice: how do they figure in?"

Roger replies, "Honestly, it feels to me like they're just sounds we make. They don't feel to me like they have any reality at all. I've picked up a pair of words, Eros and Thanatos. They seem real to me. Eros is vitality, the will to live, sexuality, raw aliveness itself; Thanatos is just death, the extinguishing of the fire, nothingness, the eternal void. Everything real is one or the other; reality is a mixture of the two."

The two men are quiet again. After a while, they get into the park vehicle, and Ted drives them over to watch Roger the male T-rex finishing up his own breakfast in peace and safety. Like Dorothy, he too eats greedily and with great gusto.

* * * * * * * * * * *

Roger drives back to his hotel after the morning's visit to Cretaceous World. He has the penthouse on top of the all-suite resort.

He pops a blue pill into his mouth as he enters the lobby. He swallows with a little difficulty and looks around the public area of the hotel.

He's searching for something, a certain someone, no one in particular really, no one he knows, just someone he needs now.

He finds her. There she is. Good, very good.

She's sitting in the restaurant. She's drinking coffee while she reads a magazine on her digital tablet. She's been waiting for something, a certain someone, no one in particular really.

She has long, thick black hair that cascades down her back in luscious waves. The pallor of her skin is striking. She's wearing a form-fitting black top with a plunging neckline.

He walks over to her table and looks her directly in the eye.

She's not alarmed. This is what she was waiting for.

She looks him in the eye too, and the ghost of a smile appears at the corners of her mouth.

He asks, "Around the world?"

She nods slightly and names a stratospheric price.

He says, "Fine, but for that much I want to orbit a couple times at least."

She shrugs but doesn't look away.

He knows this means yes.

She rises from the table and puts her tablet back into her large black purse which she throws over her left shoulder where it hangs by its strap.

He takes hold of her right arm as if arresting her.

That trace of a smile appears at the corners of her lips again. She offers no resistance.

He forcefully takes her to the elevator and pushes the up button.

He tells her, "I want to call you Dorothy."

She says, "You can call me anything you want."

He keeps his firm grip on her upper arm. The elevator door opens. He takes her into the elevator and up to the penthouse.

On the way up, he can feel the blue pill starting to work.

He thinks, "Oh yeah, a couple orbits, at least."

ARMOR

I t probably isn't necessary, but we don't take any chances.

The bony club on the end of an Ankylosaur's tail is massive enough to crack the shinbone or foot of a mighty T-rex and bring the would-be predator crashing down to the ground screaming and gnashing the dust with its crushing teeth.

The Ankylosaur's tail itself is rigid, made of fused vertebrae, so the heavy club on the end can be held always off the ground, ever ready to strike a terrible blow.

Ankylosaurs are solitary creatures. Their fossils are found individually, not in groups. They'll graze along peacefully on low vegetation like a modern rhinoceros, but if something gets close to them, they can become as belligerent as a rhino and lash out at whatever it is.

They can surely tell if the thing near them is another Ankylosaur. Of all the dinosaurs, the Ankylosaurs have left us the best fossil skulls, since their heads are so thoroughly armored. We have a very clear picture of the shape of their brains, and we know that the area dedicated to smell is very large.

Still, the Ankylosaur brain is overall very small. They're definitely not thinkers. Since they aren't gregarious by nature, they might just strike out at even a fellow Ankylosaur who has come too close.

When the fragrance of sex is in the air, then that's different, of course.

Otherwise, it's prudent for us not to encourage them to get too close to each other.

So as I say, we don't take any chances. When we feed them we leave two separate piles of food, which is what Bud and Billy have done on this already hot morning in July 2119.

They've expertly used the two big cranes thirty yards apart to lower the separate piles of food into the pen. Each pile contains several tons of mixed horsetails and ferns.

Bud has taught Billy well and has let him do the work today with both of the cranes.

Bud jokes, "I like to supervise."

I praise, "You've done a good job bringing Billy along."

Young Billy stands there happily and deferentially.

I say to Billy, "Nice job with the crane. You're getting the hang of that."

He nods and thanks me.

About this time, the first of the Ankylosaurs shows up.

Their keen sense of smell tells them the food has arrived in their pen, but they're very slow. Even though their pen is very small, two miles by two miles, it still takes them a long while to get here.

The second Ankylosaur shows up, smells where the first one is, and goes to the other pile of delicious ferns and horsetails, supplied to us fresh by nearby Cretaceous Gardens, the nursery we depend on to feed our herbivorous dinosaurs.

We three just stand and watch in silence. No matter how many years you're here at Cretaceous World, the sight of a full-grown dinosaur living and breathing right in front of you just never gets old.

This is the most armored of all the dinosaurs. A shield of bony plates, knobs, spikes, and spines embedded in the skin of an Ankylosaur protects its back, flanks, tail, neck, and head. Thirty feet long and weighing ten thousand pounds, six feet wide and four feet high, they're low and ponderous with massive gut. They flourished right up to the end of the Cretaceous, sharing habitat with Hadrosaurs and Triceratops. Being solitary, they occupied the margins, often including dry areas and mountains. They were quadrupedal browsers with head typically down, eating what grew close to the ground. They had a broad beak with long tongue and leaflike teeth inside big cheeks. Their short necks and legs made it hard for a T-rex or Albertosaur to find a place to do damage before the monstrous club on the end of the Ankylosaur's tail shattered the attacker's foot.

I watch them munching contentedly on the horsetails and ferns, and I envy them a little. I'm feeling these days like I'd love to have a suit of armor to shield me from the world. I'd love to just keep my head down and nibble along through the rest of my life.

* * * * * * * * * * * *

In the afternoon, I plod on my 69-year-old legs down to the office where Lana is explaining our record-keeping to Clark Turner, our new hire. I'm imagining I'm an Ankylosaur as I lumber through the door. I'm careful my tail-club doesn't smash the doorframe.

I say in salutation, "Greetings, Dr. Gable, Dr. Turner."

Lana smiles, "Good day, Dr. Beebe."

Clark grins, "Howdy, Ted."

So right away, we're Ted, Lana, and Clark, three people working together to run Cretaceous World. I like his attitude.

He's a tall, wiry fellow with gray appearing along the sides of this short black hair. I know from reading his job application that he's 48 years old. He still looks like he could hop up onto a quarter horse and round up stray steers after a thunderstorm. As I learned from his interview during the hiring process, he used to do exactly that while growing up on a ranch in Montana.

One look at Lana tells me she's comfortable with this full Professor from the University of Colorado who is fifteen years her senior. They're both paleontologists, and that helps. Being a microbiologist myself, I'm always kind of winging it with dinosaurs. I've noticed that sometimes Lana is a bit impatient with what I don't know about the anatomical characteristics of various dinosaur clades and about the geology and climate of the Mesozoic. She's kind to me and tries not to show her momentary impatience, but I do notice.

Seeing the two of them together, I feel my late Becky by my side again, and I sense myself fading into the shadows with her. Becky and I are the past. It's obvious now. These two, Lana and Clark, who seem like kids to me, they're the future of our grand project, Becky's and mine. At least, I hope they are. That would be great. I really want this to work out, so I can stop worrying about what's to come for our baby, this place dedicated to dinosaurs.

I ask Clark, "So how's it going in general? Any trouble in settling in? I'm here to smooth the way."

He says, "Going well. I'm loving it living in a town of dinosaurs. I'd like to have a meeting with you in a week or so, after I get oriented. I'd like to talk further about the direction I want to take the museum here at the park. I'm pretty excited about the potential for it to be a world-class facility, unique because of its proximity to these amazing reconstructions of dinosaurs based on what the actual fossils have taught us."

I say, "Any time. Door's always open. Let me know when you're ready."

I like his phrase, "a town of dinosaurs." Human life here is organized around them and economically depends on human fascination with them. Our benefactor and founder, Randy Winston, is rich enough and generous enough that we don't have to base our decisions and actions on the profit motive. We make enough on the worldwide mail-order demand for our dinosaur T-shirts, pajamas, videos, action-figures, coffee cups, and various other dino paraphernalia to keep us in the black, which is all Randy asks us to do. We have no pressure to do anything else but follow our purest motives in making decisions about the park.

We don't aim to please the crowd. You come here, you're patient, you're lucky, and you see some dinosaurs. The experience acquires and retains its value.

Maybe at that point it occurs to you that sixty-five million years from now, there won't be any humans, odds are. We come, we go: from nothing to nothing again, so far as we can tell. Once you get past the terror of that realization, once you accept the limits of our situation, serenity becomes possible, and if you're really lucky, wisdom. That's what our town of dinosaurs is here for.

I feel death close to me now, watching my every move, waiting for the moment for my passing.

I make a mental note to tell Lana later that I'm an Ankylosaur, armored against the slings and arrows of outrageous Fortune, a bony club on the end of my tail to use against a league of troubles.

Lana asks me, "Did you enjoy yourself at the Ankylosaur pen this morning?"

I say, "Sure did. By the way, Bud has brought Billy along to where he's a whiz with the cranes now."

Clark says, "*Ankylosaurus magniventris*, I excavated three of them in Montana in the Hell Creek Formation. Their armor is so extensive, their skeletons tend to be really well preserved. It was a joy digging them up. Their skulls were perfectly intact. I felt like the gravedigger in *Hamlet*."

I laugh, "Alas, poor Yorick."

He says, "I actually did say that. Each time with each one of them."

Lana laughs, "A fellow of no jest or fancy, he hath borne me on his back a thousand times."

Clark and I chuckle.

Clark says, "Very good. I'll have to remember that the next time I'm digging one up."

Then Lana says, "Excuse me, gentlemen. As the female of the species, I must go pump some milk, lest I begin to leak."

She's left little Fred in the nursery here on the second floor together with several bottles of her own breast milk.

She adds, "I'll be back shortly, twenty minutes or so," and off she goes with some haste into the bathroom.

Lana and I've turned one of the many general purpose rooms in the sprawling residence into a nursery, and we leave Fred there often. We've placed a long-term employee there, Juana, whom we trust implicitly, having done a thorough background check all the way back to her infancy in Woodburn. We've doubled her salary and asked her to be available any time day or night seven days a week. If she becomes ill, her backup is Mona, also thoroughly checked out and also receiving more salary just to be available if and whenever Juana can't do the job. Despite the implicitness of the aforementioned trust, we also video-record everything that happens in the nursery and have our security department check it over on a regular basis, just to be totally sure nothing wrong is being done around or to our little Fred.

While Lana is away expressing milk, Clark and I chat a bit. He's a quiet fellow, taciturn even, but he opens up readily if you show interest in something he's obsessed by. He's also quite a good listener if you want to tell him about something scientific you're obsessed with. I find him easy to talk to.

Before long, he's telling me, "I'm glad to be away from the classroom. I've always preferred the museum and the dig site. The classroom has always seemed confining to me. In a museum analyzing and classifying the results of an excavation or else out in the field doing the actual digging, those are the places where I feel free."

I tell him I was glad to leave teaching behind in order actually to do something in the world for a change.

He says, "Teaching is pushing the same boulder up the hill over and over again. The new students show up every year not knowing the same things that the previous students didn't know. It's important work and was rewarding the first few years, but then it got to be a grind. Compared to being out in a beautiful spot in Montana or Colorado discovering the remains of an amazing creature from a hundred million years ago, or to being in a museum lab identifying parts and assembling the structure of that creature, the classroom becomes dull as jail after a while."

I mention that in my field you don't really get to dig up single cells from two or three billion years ago, unfortunately. What a thrill that would be. Also, bacteria and protists don't make very impressive museum exhibits.

I joke, "I don't think Precambrian Park would be as successful as Cretaceous World has been."

He laughs, and a sincere gleam of amusement shines in his green eyes.

Lana returns with a couple bottles of breast milk which she puts in the small refrigerator that Becky bought so lunches and refreshments could be kept in the office.

I say ta-tá to Lana and Clark and make my way upstairs to the master bedroom on the third floor for a nice little nap.

* * * * * * * * * * * *

It's evening, and we're gathered around the dinner table in our private dining room, Lana, Fred, and I. Lana is breast-feeding Fred, and I'm eating spaghetti. Lana is also spoon-feeding him some baby rice mashed in breast milk, and I'm also having some blueberries and grape juice.

Fred is seven months old now and weighs over twenty pounds. He's begun to imitate sounds we make, which I'm told is a bit precocious of him. He says "mama" and "papa," though he doesn't attach these words to Lana and me.

Fred becomes full and dozes off. Lana takes him into our bedroom and puts him in the crib to sleep. She comes back into our private kitchen and dining area and dishes herself a plate of spaghetti. She sits down across the table from me and starts eating.

I say, "I really identified with the Ankylosaurs this morning."

She guesses, "Because they speak softly and carry a big stick?"

I say, "Very funny. Yes, that and because I feel armored against the slings and arrows of outrageous Fortune."

She suddenly looks sad.

I comment, "I somehow thought you'd find that funny. Shows how astute at predicting I am. I suppose you feel that I wouldn't be closed off to the world if I really loved you."

She nods.

I tell her earnestly, "I do love you. Very much. Please believe me."

She smiles with resignation.

She says, "I know you do. You're still married to Becky in your heart, though. I understand. Really, I do. I'll cheer up now. It was just a passing twinge of regret."

I smile tenderly.

I think, "You keep living: you see what happens."

I ask, "So how'd it go with Clark today?"

She says, "Well, I gave up any idea of his taking over any of the work in the office."

I say, "Really? Hmm."

She says, "It was obvious he wasn't going to accept doing that sort of thing. I didn't want to scare him back to Boulder. He's on a year-long leave of absence, you know. His old teaching job is waiting for him to go back to if he doesn't like it here."

She chews and swallows.

She says, "We should hire a bookkeeper. The rest I can do myself. I'm good at keeping track and checking on things. I kind of like doing it. I'm a born observer. We should leave Clark free to focus on his museum."

I say, "Yes, it doesn't take long to see that the only reason Clark's here is because he sees it as a unique opportunity to develop a great museum. That and because he was single and you thought he was cute."

She laughs, "What can I say? So I've got a daddy thing. So shoot me."

I laugh, "Okay, I'll shoot you."

She gives me the look.

She says, "Might I suggest you squish me instead? I'm in the mood for a good squishing."

I'm still taking the pills.

I ask, "What about Fred? Won't we wake him up? We need the bed for a proper squishing."

Squishing is our little term for the classic missionary position. She's a natural bottom, and I'm a natural top, so we both really enjoy the squishing.

She says, "Don't be silly."

She puts down her fork and takes me by the hand. She leads me into our private living room and over to the big, extra-long sofa in there.

She says, "Use your imagination, Dr. Beebe."

So I do.

PALEOBUGS

Martin sits on the banks of the Illahee and observes. He's come here in January 2120 when it's cool and pleasant in the morning. The temperature is an agreeable 70 degrees at 8 a.m. today.

Ted is sitting on Martin's left, and Lana on his right. They've conducted him down here to the western edge of Cretaceous World because he requested it. He wants to be beside the river for hours and days to contemplate the insect life there.

Martin Jones is the world's leading paleoentomologist, and Ted and Lana run Cretaceous World. They're his hosts here at the world-famous dinosaur park. He's come to this place that now in 2120 so closely resembles a riparian forest in the Cretaceous era. He hopes to see some things in the insect life here that will help him to understand even better the paleobugs he's spent his entire adult life assiduously studying.

Martin says, "It's so easy to imagine seeing a Pachycephalosaur moving along this stream and a group of Triceratops ambling through the ferns and evergreen trees, maybe with an Ankylosaur grazing in a quiet spot out of everybody's way."

Lana agrees, "It really is. I often picture ornithopods and sauropods in this setting. It just seems natural to do so."

Ted adds, "Perhaps a few hungry theropods are lurking about, searching for the opportunity to attack."

Martin says, "The carnivores hunt the herbivores, except I think it's really more accurate to call the latter omnivores, because they eat a lot of bugs as they chomp down their daily vegetation. A Hadrosaur or Iguanodon, for example, might be looking for a lot of plants to eat, but they'll also wind up consuming many helpings of caterpillars, beetles, aphids, and other arthropods in the process."

Ted observes, "So, no fossils exist to speak of for Mesozoic bugs or plants. Makes it tough to study them, does it not?"

Martin explains, "Well, there really is a lot of evidence preserved in amber. We can tell a huge amount from the insects, arachnids, plants, and fungi trapped in the clear tree resin."

Lana says, "I should pay more attention to the amber record. There aren't any large dinosaurs preserved in amber, so I just haven't focused much on it."

Martin says, "If you're an entomologist, it's the best thing there is. You've got a real treasure trove: scarab beetles, dung beetles, rove beetles, phorid flies, planthoppers, aphids, thrips, whiteflies, gall gnats, leafhoppers, scale insects, crickets, long-horned grasshoppers, palm beetles, wasps, moths, flower beetles, weevils, both winged and wingless ants, cockroaches, termites, pygmy grasshoppers, caddis flies, sand flies, bees, biting midges, biting flies, primitive crane flies, lake flies, scorpion flies, mosquitoes of course, mites, and so on and on and on."

Ted and Lana smile at their guest's ability to produce such a long list of examples off the top of his expert head.

Martin adds, "We can even see tiny parasitic worms emerging from host insect bodies."

Ted probes, "I don't suppose there's much for us microbiologists in the amber."

Martin replies, "There is. There are cysts of protozoans that cause dysentery, for instance."

Lana says, "I seldom think of bugs when I think of dinosaurs."

Martin admits, "I have a very hard time thinking of dinosaurs without imagining the critters that torment them and afflict them with disease. I always picture dinosaurs tortured by horseflies, fleas, ticks, mosquitoes, and many other little demons together with the parasites and diseases they transmit: the roundworms, lungworms, nematodes, heartworms, eyeworms, tapeworms, flatworms, malarial protozoans, bacterial infections, viruses, and others of this ilk."

Lana is saddened by this thought but says nothing.

Ted offers, "If it helps, the vast majority of bacterial beings are beneficial, even necessary for the health and happiness of larger life-forms. That's the thought that kept me cheerful back when I was an academic up to my eyeballs in the study of prokaryotes. This was long ago in my life before Cretaceous World."

Martin responds blandly, "Thanks. I'll try to keep that in mind. Maybe it will make me a bit less melancholy about dinosaurs and their lot in life."

* * * * * * * * * * * *

Little Martin was sitting on the couch in his parents' home. His mother's lover was sitting there with him. They were waiting for Martin's mother to come home from wherever she was.

Martin's father was living on another continent. He hadn't been home in over two years. He hadn't been home more than two years total in the last ten. He remained married to Martin's mother though. Neither of them wanted a divorce. They were both comfortable with their arrangement and didn't rule out living together again someday.

Martin missed his father very much. He often thought about him and went over his memories of him in every detail again and again. Not that there were all that many of them, the memories of daddy. The old boy really hadn't been home with mommy all that much during little Martin's lifetime.

Martin liked to talk with the men who came to see his mother. It filled the hole in his heart a little bit for a little while.

The middle-aged man beside Martin on the couch was named Arthur.

Arthur asked Martin, "Does your mom ever say anything to you about me?"

Martin answered, "No. Not much."

Art pursued, "So she does say something. Come on, tell me what she says. Be my friend. You're my friend, aren't you?"

Martin smiled. He liked the idea that he was Arthur's friend.

Martin said, "She just says you're nice. She says she has fun with you."

Art was pleased.

Martin said, "I asked mommy if she likes your beard."

Arthur asked, "What did she say?"

Martin replied, "She said it's scratchy on her face right after you trim it. She said she thinks it looks good though."

Art chuckled.

He asked, "What do you think?"

Martin said, "I like it because it reminds me of daddy's beard."

Art's face went blank.

He asked, "Do you see your daddy? I mean, do you go stay with him? He doesn't come here, does he?"

Martin lied, "Yes, I see him a lot. Not here though. I go to his other house and stay with him for a while. Sometimes mommy comes with me and stays there too."

Arthur asked, "So he never stays here? Not in this house?"

Martin continued to invent the father he wanted, "Oh no, he stays here sometimes. He's here sometimes. We sit on this couch and talk sometimes. We do things together, lots of things."

Art sensed this wasn't true. He'd been seeing Martin's mother long enough to know it wasn't likely, and he felt the boy's sudden self-contradiction gave him away.

He said, "I'm happy for you."

He felt sad for little Martin.

He asked, "Do other men come here to see your mommy?"

Martin replied innocently, "Yes. Lots."

Art expressed surprise, "Lots?"

Martin nodded his head yes.

He said, "Phil and Bill, Jack and Jerry, Tim and Greg. Lots."

Arthur asked, "They come in pairs?"

Martin answered, "No. I just remember them that way. I don't know why."

Little Martin was exaggerating. These men weren't all still visiting his mother. He just wished they were. He'd liked talking with them, and then they were gone, never to return.

Art was suddenly very pensive. He believed the boy about these other lovers. Maybe it was the jealousy that always lurked in the background, but he did believe him. He felt sure the boy was lying about his father, yet he trusted what he said about these other men still visiting here.

Little Martin tried to continue the conversation, but Arthur gave terse answers and brooded.

Finally, Martin's mother came home. She hugged him and kissed him on the cheek.

Art took mommy in another room and closed the door. They began to argue. After some yelling, Arthur stormed out, slamming the front door behind him.

Little Martin knew the man wouldn't be back. Mommy wouldn't forgive men who yelled at her. Once a man yelled at mommy, he never came to the house again. Mommy wouldn't let him.

Martin was numb. He began imagining another visit by Arthur.

He began inventing the things he would say to Arthur. He began imagining the things he'd like Art to say to him.

* * * * * * * * * * * *

Ted stands and says, "We'd better head back to the barn."

Lana stands up too.

Ted asks Martin, "You going to be all right here alone? Is there anything we can do for you?"

Martin replies, "I'm fine. I'll find my own way out. Just follow the gravel road to the front gate, right?"

Ted confirms, "That's it. Give us a call if you run into any problems. We won't be far away."

Lana says, "You know, we don't have any dinosaurs running around here by the river, but we do have some fairly big mammals lurking about. Do you have a defense against black bears and mountain lions?"

Martin affirms, "Oh yes, I'm packing. Not a gun, but the most powerful bear and cougar repellent known to modern science. I've got a couple spray canisters of it. It's kept me safe in remote sites all over the West."

Ted and Lana go to their vehicle and leave.

As the two of them drive away, Lana says, "There's something off-kilter about that guy."

Ted agrees, "He's definitely a glass-half-empty kind of thinker."

Lana continues, "He's negative. He sees sickness and death wherever he looks."

Ted observes, "You know, the fossil record is so scanty, and the amber record even scantier, that it becomes a sort of Rorschach test: we tend to see in it what we're predisposed to perceive."

Meanwhile back on the riverbank, the world's leading paleoentomologist begins to visualize scenes here in which paleobugs afflict or infect dinosaurs in the Cretaceous.

He sees a group of Hadrosaurs grazing on the ferns. Suddenly, masses of sand flies engulf them, rising from resting places on the bark of trees and savagely biting the defenseless herbivores.

He sees an ailing Ankylosaur, obviously in pain. He imagines that there are masses of roundworms in its bulging stomach. The eggs of the roundworms pass in the dinosaur's dung. Cockroaches and beetles then feed on these feces and ingest the worms' eggs as they do so.

When other dinosaurs eat these insects, they become infected with the roundworms too.

He sees a Pachycephalosaur moving among the horsetails, eating as it goes. A tick waits patiently for the right moment and attaches itself to the dinosaur. It crawls with its short front legs to an area of soft tissue around the ear opening and inserts a barbed tube through which it then takes its blood meal.

He sees an Iguanodon feeding on ferns. A large horsefly begins circling its head, searching for a safe place to land on its skin. When it finds one, it lands and uses its powerful mouth to gash an opening. The intense pain makes the Iguanodon stop eating and try to drive away the horsefly. A giant crocodilian is watching from the water. A second horsefly bites the Iguanodon on the hind leg, and it wades into the river, trying to make the flies get off. The soaking does dislodge the horsefly on its leg, but vise-like crocodilian teeth suddenly clamp down on its haunch and drag it under the surface of the river with much thrashing. The Iguanodon likely wouldn't have fallen prey today if the horseflies hadn't distracted it.

He sees the mighty T-rex hunting here, watching some Hadrosaurs feeding on water lilies. Suddenly, a famished cloud of blackflies descends on the colossal predator and seeks out soft spots in its skin. Sharp mandibles penetrate by the hundreds, and maddened by the searing pain, the T-rex goes crashing into the forest. Stumbling over boulders and the trunks of fallen evergreens, the desperate brute risks a broken leg that might cause it to starve to death.

He sees several Triceratops browsing peacefully in an idyllic glade. A battalion of hungry biting midges rises from some nearby reeds like a puff of dark smoke. The bulky dinosaurs feel many jabs of sharp pain as the tiny midges find soft vulnerable spots on their skin. After three minutes or so, the midges finish feeding on the blood of the dinosaurs. The pain stops, but the ceratopsians have now been infected with microscopic parasites that will weaken them and shorten their lives.

Martin enjoys these visualizations of his. He doesn't find them gloomy or depressing because he sides with the insects and revels in their victories over the much larger creatures.

He remains on the riverbank until the sun goes down. Then he returns to the hotel in neighboring Dewberry, has dinner alone in his hotel room, and goes to bed early. He sleeps soundly through the night. When he wakes, he's refreshed. He tries to remember any dreams he had, but he can't.

BELLY

I say, "The big spike at thumb position: that's why the food's in two piles."

Clark asks, "You think they might use the thumb-spikes on each other?"

I reply, "Well, we had them designed so they'd use the spikes for cracking open fruit and seed pods, but we don't really know they won't use them for defense and for settling rivalry disputes."

He adds, "Like we believe they actually did back in the early Cretaceous."

We're standing on a vantage point that overlooks the Iguanodon pen. It's feeding time for our two Iguanodons, and we two humans are watching them eat. Several tons of horsetails, ferns, and gingko leaves have been dumped into the pen in two piles using the giant crane that's located near where we're standing.

Even though Clark's focused on the fossil museum here at Cretaceous World, I want him to get to know the rest of the operation. I want him to meet the people who do the daily work, like Bud and Billy, the crane operators who feed the dinosaurs, and all the other people who make the place hum. I want Clark to become familiar with the whole structure of the organization and see how it works as an organism. He's quite happy to do this. Who wouldn't be?

Clark asks, "So how big is the Iguanodon area?"

I say, "Ten by seven miles. These guys are very mobile. They need some elbow room."

We continue watching these amazing creatures as they munch contentedly in this mid-morning in March 2120.

Bud and Billy have gone on to the next feeding area on their schedule. They'll use the truck and crane to place species-appropriate food inside the walls of the pen there as they did here. They also use a catapult to hurl sheep carcasses into the pens of our carnivores. We prefer sheep to cattle and pigs because mature cattle and pigs are too big.

They're unwieldy on the catapult. Also, pigs are too smart. It seems wrong to use them for food if we don't have to. Young cattle would work, but that seems wrong too. We've settled on mature sheep as our normal Theropod food. Never lambs, of course. That too offends our moral sensibility.

Clark and I are alone together.

He says, "Iguanodon was one of the first two dinosaurs named. It was named before the term 'dinosaur' even existed."

I look at him with curiosity.

He continues, "Gideon Mantell, a family doctor, and his wife Mary Ann, they were amateur fossil enthusiasts in Southern England during the early nineteenth century. They came to possess some interesting fossil teeth which they thought were very like those of the modern Iguana lizards, only much bigger. They decided the fossil teeth belonged to a long-extinct plant-eating lizard, which in 1825 they named Iguanodon, 'Iguana-tooth.' It wasn't until sixteen years later in 1841 that Sir Richard Owen saw fit to create the larger term Dinosauria, 'great and fearsome reptiles,' which included the Iguanodon."

Dr. Clark Turner may not know as much about the first three billion years of life on Earth as a microbiologist like me does, but it's impressive the details he does know about the most recent 250 million years, especially about the Jurassic and Cretaceous and about the people in modern times who have studied the Mesozoic.

I look at the mouths of these two Iguanodon facsimiles before us. The front of the mouth is a toothless beak, narrow and rounded. The long cheeks cover the tall, ridged teeth at the rear of the mouth. They're about the size of elephants, fifteen feet tall and four tons in weight. The tail of the Iguanodon is much bigger than an elephant's, of course, so they're about thirty feet long. Unlike elephants, they can move about on their two rear limbs almost as well as on all fours. In fact, they're basically bipedal when juveniles and only become more quadrupedal when they mature and put on weight. The thin, tuberculate skin covers a huge belly, very similar to the Hadrosaur's.

I say, "I like to imagine great herds of these Ornithopods roaming the wetlands of what's now Northern Europe, grazing on horsetail beds, gorging on gingko leaves, eating ferns along the edges of the marshes."

Clark says, "Yes, they're definitely built for gorging. Look at those bellies. I've personally found bone-beds and fossilized mud trackways

that show the Iguanodons existed in great numbers in the early Cretaceous. The rise of the angiosperms produced more food more quickly
and seems to have favored the Iguanodons over many of the giant Sauropods."

The bellies make me think of Lana. She's six months pregnant
again. This time it's not my doing. She's had the little girl in her belly
DNA-tested already and knows that it's Clark's child.

I say, "The belly, yes, the belly."

He turns and looks at me.

I say, "The baby's fine with me, Clark. I just wanted to tell you
that. I hope you don't mind my saying so. I know you don't need my
approval, but I wanted you to know you have it nevertheless."

Clark looks down. We're silent for a moment. The Iguanodons
keep munching, filling their big bellies even fuller.

Clark says, "We've been tiptoeing around that for quite a while."

I agree, "It's been the 8,000-pound dinosaur in the room."

He laughs.

I wait.

He says, "Lana asked me when I was going to make an honest
woman of her."

I say, "I'm familiar with the question."

He says, "Yes, she mentioned that."

I observe, "She can be remarkably straightforward."

He concurs, "Yes, she can."

We both look down and smile.

He says, "So I asked her to marry me."

I look up and say, "I didn't know."

He reveals, "She said yes."

I look down and say, "Of course. Congratulations. Really, I mean
it sincerely."

We look each other in the eye and shake hands firmly.

From somewhere nearby, a Steller's jay imitates a red-tailed hawk.
Cheeky little dinosaur.

* * * * * * * * * * *

In the afternoon, I'm with Lana in the cavernous living room of our
quarters atop the residence. I suppose by "our" I now mean Becky's
and mine only. Now more than ever, because Lana's engaged to an-

other man and spends her nights with him not me.

I say, "Clark asked me about Velociraptors and Deinonychus today."

She asks, "While you were watching the Iguanodons eat this morning?"

I respond, "Yeah, he was just wondering if we had any plans to add some of the better-known smallish dinosaurs to our array."

She smirks.

I observe, "You smirk."

She says, "No comment."

I inquire, "Really?"

She laughs, "Well, when they make a movie about us, they can add some Velociraptors and Deinonychus so they can have an exciting disaster scene when the 'raptors' inevitably get loose."

I say, "That's basically what I told him."

She says, "Nothing but great big dinosaurs for us. Nobody who can jump or climb over any barriers."

We smile at each other.

We're sitting on comfortable sofas on opposite sides of the magnificent mahogany coffee table. Her belly is pushing her blouse out impressively.

I stop smiling and say, "Clark told me he's going to make an honest woman of you."

She says, "Well, you wouldn't. Somebody's got to do it."

I declare, "I'm happy for you. Sincerely. I'll do everything I can to make this work."

She smiles, "I know you will. I love you, but you still love Becky. It's like something out of Shakespeare: Robin Goodfellow has made this mischief."

I ask, "Does Clark love you?"

She replies, "No, Puck hasn't applied the magic juice to his eyes."

I continue, "And yet he proposes marriage, and you accept?"

She snorts, "Love belongs in the back seat of a convertible. Marriage is a practical, legal contract."

I comment, "Tough cookie."

She expands, "Clark is a responsible guy. He likes me, and he likes my son. He'll make a good husband and a good father. He isn't looking for love. Up till now, he's been satisfying his sexual needs with female colleagues and admiring graduate students. Marriage would've just gotten in the way of his focus on his research. Here, it's different. I can satisfy his sexual needs, and marriage to me solidifies his position here and his focus on developing the fossil museum."

I remark, "A dynastic marriage, a political alliance."

She looks me in the eye, "I can take care of your sexual needs too, grandpa. You seem to me a most discreet gentleman. Clark doesn't care about that sort of thing. So long as we're seemly and don't embarrass or inconvenience him, he won't even think about it."

I say, "You're a real Bonobo, you know. What are you building here, a primate matriarchy?"

She nods yes.

She comes over to where I'm sitting on a sofa and kneels before me.

I uncross my legs. I know what she wants to do.

She unzips my pants and puts me in her mouth. Big as her belly is, she has no trouble remaining in position until I eventually release a little magic love juice into her soft, warm orifice.

* * * * * * * * * * * *

It's night, and I'm talking to Becky. We're lying side by side in bed, facing each other. The lamp is on.

I say, "I was sitting at the bottom of a dry well."

She asks, "How did you get there?"

I say, "I must have climbed down somehow."

She asks, "How? Was there a ladder? Or a rope?"

I say, "No, there was no obvious easy way to get down there."

She adds, "Or to get back up."

I agree, "Right. I was stuck down there. I'm not even sure it was once a well. I'm not sure what it was."

She asks, "Was it clean?"

I reply, "As clean as dirt and rock can be."

She infers, "So there was no brick or concrete lining to it."

I respond, "None. It was just a perfectly cylindrical hole in the ground."

She asks, "How deep was it?"

I say, "It was deep. I don't know how deep. I could still see the top of the hole high above me, so I guess it wasn't too deep."

She asks, "Was it dark?"

I say, "Yes, but the round mouth of the hole way up there was a small, bright light. Yet the light from it didn't reach me there at the bottom. I was in the dark."

She wonders anxiously, "Had you fallen in? Were you hurt?"

I reassure her, "Nope. I was fine. Not a scratch."

She asks, "Was there anything else there with you in the hole? A mammal or insect or whatever?"

I expand, "There was only about a googleplex of creatures down there with me, living in the walls of the hole. I expect I was deep enough to be down at the level of the unweathered rock. Above me probably were layers of the soil, the result of biological beings working on the parent material. Thousands of types of bacteria were living in those upper layers. There were many micro-arthropods. Springtails and mites abounded, as did non-arthropods like the microscopic water bears. Up near the top of the hole, the earthworms turned the fallen leaves into dirt. The roots of trees and other plants spread out up there. They had no intention of coming down where I was. They stayed up near the surface where the soil was richest and the rainwater most abundant. The mycorrhizae were up there too, breaking the triple covalent bonds of the nitrogen molecules and introducing usable nitrogen atoms into the food chain for the building of genes and proteins. Trillions of creatures lived above where I was: salamanders, fly and beetle larvae, ants, spiders, centipedes, moles, voles, nematodes, protozoa, and so on and on, all alive above me. I was sitting in the dark basement of life on Earth. Below me a couple hundred miles or so was the still radioactive, semi-molten and fully molten star-stuff that's the overwhelming majority of our planet's mass."

She asks, "So what did you do?"

I reveal, "I took a nap."

She repeats, "You took a nap."

I explain, "Yes, I took a nap, and when I woke up, I was out of the hole."

She says, "Just like that."

I affirm, "Yep, just like that. I was up on the surface lying beside the mouth of the dry well or just plain hole or whatever it was."

Becky just looks at me and smiles.

I say, "You're looking younger these days."

She just keeps smiling tenderly.

I say, "So that's when things got really strange."

She asks, "That wasn't the strange part you just told me?"

I reply, "Not at all. Listen to this. The sun had just gone below the horizon. The sky was pale blue. I looked up and saw the ghostly Moon overhead. It was huge. It seemed much closer to Earth than usual. It seemed to be cracked along a line running from north to south."

She questions, "Cracked?"

I explain, "Yeah, cracked, you know, a big wide crack appeared on its face and ran all the way from top to bottom, like it was cracking in half."

She asks, "So what happened?"

I say, "Well, I looked around me, thinking I needed to find a place to hide. I was spooked."

She waits. Her eyes grow bigger.

I continue, "When I looked up again at the Moon, it was even closer, and more cracks had appeared on its surface. A huge chunk was breaking off from its upper left quadrant. The whole Moon was coming apart, and before long big pieces of it were going to be striking the Earth with cataclysmic force. I could jump back in the dry well or hole or whatever, and it wouldn't do me any good. There was nowhere to hide."

Her eyes are huge now, and her mouth is hanging open a little.

I say, "I looked around me again, and now there were people everywhere. They were just strolling happily around. They weren't worried at all. They were blissfully oblivious to the doom that was upon them. By now there were several more huge pieces of Moon that had come apart and were rushing towards the surface of Earth. I wanted to run somewhere, I wanted desperately to escape, but there was nowhere to go."

She asks, "So that was it, the end?"

I say, "Not exactly. Suddenly I had in hand a copy of Paradise Lost in German by Johannes Milton and was trying my best to understand it. Then I noticed that there was a murder mystery being played out inside the extensive critical apparatus around the poem, so I tried to solve that."

Becky laughs loudly with pure delight.

She says, "You've dreamed the beginning of the Anthropocene, my love."

I wake up suddenly. I'm alone in bed. The lamp is off, and Becky is gone.

I think, "I'm so glad I can still talk with Becky in my dreams. I

know if I started another marriage, she wouldn't come to see me anymore. Gradually, she'd come less and less often and then finally not at
all. I'll do anything not to lose her completely. I need her so much."

BONES

Nigel says, "Thank you for giving me a tour of the museum. It's very impressive what you're doing here."

Clark responds, "My pleasure. I'm so glad we persuaded you to pay us a visit."

Nigel Rathbone is the Keeper of the Fossil Collections at the British Museum of Paleontology. He's flown all the way from London, England, here to Western Oregon to see the Fossil Museum at Cretaceous World. Clark Turner is the Director of the museum, which is now undergoing a major expansion and which is soon to be renamed the Turner Museum of the Mesozoic in Clark's honor.

Clark suggests, "I feel like we could do each other a lot of good if we decided to."

Nigel says, "You pique my curiosity, sir. Pray tell me the details."

Clark explains, "As I see things, we have complementary needs and capabilities. My museum, on the one hand, wants to add to its collection of the spinosaurids. We'd like to acquire Baryonyx and Suchosaurus from Britain; Suchomimus, Cristatusaurus, and Ostafrikasaurus from Africa; Irritator and Oxalaia from Brazil; and Ichthyovenator and Siamosaurus from Southeast Asia. It would of course be wonderful to have another African Spinosaur as well.

"Your museum, on the other hand, wants to acquire more complete examples of the dinosaurs of Western America: Triceratops, T-rex, Albertosaur, Parasaurolophus, Edmontosaur, Stegosaur, Ankylosaur, Iguanodon, Pachycephalosaur. We're positioned to learn of opportunities for obtaining these. We fund our own digs in Colorado, Utah, Montana, Alberta, and know of digs there that are backed by others.

"It occurs to me that you would be similarly well-positioned to know of digs for spinosaurids in Britain, in Africa, and because of your proximity to France, in Southeast Asia. I feel confident we could help each other significantly to fulfill our respective goals in collection-building."

The two middle-aged men are sitting in Clark's luxuriously furnished office on the second floor of the museum. It's almost noon on a weekday in October 2120.

Nigel considers, "Yes, it's true that the historical aftermath of the British Empire and the French colonial period leaves us in a good position to do what you suggest. I can also see how your position in North America provides you with the special opportunities you describe."

Clark proposes, "Very well then, let us form the Anglo-American Alliance for the Advancement of Cretaceous Collections."

Clark smiles.

Nigel smiles and says, "Brilliant! The quadruple A, double C. Most enjoyable. Yes, I agree to belong. Current membership, two."

* * * * * * * * * * * *

Later the same day, Clark and Nigel are sitting in the museum's Cretaceous Café. They're enjoying a very late lunch.

Nigel is beginning a story: "The Chasmosaur at the Museu Nacional in Rio recently disappeared overnight. They came in one morning, and it wasn't there anymore. It was the size of a smallish Indian elephant or a very large rhino, and yet it had simply vanished. No one had seen anything. Every fossilized bone of the anatomically complete skeleton was inexplicably missing."

Clark says, "I noticed that in the online news. It wasn't clear what happened. I couldn't really understand what was being described."

Nigel says, "No one can. It's a complete mystery. I happened to be visiting there when it happened."

Clark asks, "Any suspects?"

Nigel replies, "The night watchman disappeared on the same night, a bony old man. No one knows where he went."

Clark observes, "The fossil bones had been thoroughly described, I assume."

Nigel nods, "Of course."

Clark concludes, "So if they turn up in any museum anywhere in the world, people like you and me will recognize them as the ones missing from the collection in Rio."

Nigel nods again, "Absolutely. Few outside our profession realize that each set of fossil bones is as unique as a fingerprint. Which parts of the skeleton are missing, which parts of which bones are absent, what condition each fossilized bone is in: the pattern of all this has been created by chance destruction and is as singular as a snowflake."

Clark asserts, "Therefore, we can rule out agents of a museum as the culprits. I'm guessing a wealthy private collector somewhere in the wide world is enjoying his very own Chasmosaur in some beautiful and utterly secure spot on one of his vast, sprawling estates."

Nigel says, "By the way, our museum would very much like to obtain a fairly complete Chasmosaur. When another one is found and excavated, it will likely be fairly close to the eastern slope of the Rocky Mountains. Likewise for the Pentaceratops, the Anchiceratops, really any of the spectacularly fringed ceratopsians."

Clark promises, "I'll keep my ears alert, my eyes open, my senses keen."

Nigel smiles appreciatively.

Clark asks, "So who do you suspect stole the Chasmosaur?"

Nigel responds, "I'm rather more focused on how. I imagine that if we knew how, we should soon also know who."

Clark amends, "All right then, how?"

Nigel smiles bashfully, "I may have implied somewhat more than I can deliver. I'm focused on how, yes, but much as one focuses on a dense fog without being able to distinguish anything definite."

Clark suggests, "Maybe the bony watchman shrank the Cosmosaur and walked out with it in his pocket."

Nigel chuckles.

Clark continues, "Or maybe the Cosmosaur just vanished into thin air. After all, that's what time does to all of us, to all things, makes us, makes them all, vanish into thin air."

Nigel muses, "Where are the ceratopsians of yesteryear? That's the question. If we humans last for a million more years, maybe a couple million, we can preserve these fossil remains a bit longer, but eventually, and not that far off in geological time, they and we will have lost our form altogether and will have merged with other matter to make other forms entirely."

Clark paraphrases Candide, "*Cela est bien dit, mais il faut cultiver nos musées.*"

Nigel concurs, "Indeed. Just so."

The two museum curators finish their meal affably and part ways, one returning to his magnificent office, the other to his comfortable hotel suite in nearby Dewberry. Thus ends the inaugural meeting of the facetiously yet nobly named Anglo-American Alliance for the Advancement of Cretaceous Collections. May it long survive and prosper.

SAIL

Little Fred says, "I came to see the dinosaur that Grandpa calls the Spinosaur."

I declaim, "My grandson is a poet though he doesn't know it."

We smile. He knows it's funny, though he's not sure why. He's early in his third year of life, but he's precocious in his ability with language and says things beyond his years and understanding. Of course, it's possible I'm slightly biased.

We're watching the two Spinosaurs feast on piles of rainbow trout and leopard shark. An aquaculture business over at Yaquina Bay on the Oregon Coast supplies us with the many tons of trout and shark we need. They also sell to restaurants and local grocery stores, but we're by far their biggest customer.

Fred and I are standing side by side on the hillside overlooking the feeding area. The pen is five miles by three miles and contains large areas of marsh and pond. The Spinosaurs actually spend as much time in the water as a hippopotamus or a crocodile. The spot where our crane operator dumps the piles of fish is dry ground that can take the weight.

Lana is sitting on a blanket beside us. She's nursing baby Sue, who's seven months old now.

Lana says to Fred, "Ask Grandpa what that big thing on their back is."

Fred looks up at me and asks, "What is it, Grandpa?"

I say, "We call it a sail because that's what it looks like, the sail on a boat. It isn't really a sail though. We just call it that."

Fred asks, "What is it really?"

I say, "That's a very good question, Fred. What it is is bones that stick up and are covered with skin that stretches between the bones."

Lana says, "Ask Grandpa what it does."

I look over my shoulder at her, and she's looking back at me with a mischievous sparkle in her eyes.

Fred asks, "What's it do, Grandpa? What's the sail do?"

I say, "We're not really sure. It might help the Spinosaur to cool off. It might be something the Spinosaur likes to show off to other dinosaurs. Some people even think it might help the Spinosaur to fish by making a shadow on the water that fish like. The fish swim over to be in the shade where they feel safer, and the Spinosaur catches them."

Fred asks, "Does it eat them?"

I say, "Yes, it eats them. It loves to catch fish and eat them. There were really big fish a long time ago when there were lots of dinosaurs."

When he's a little older, I'll tell him all about the ten-foot Coelocanths, the twenty-foot sawfish, and the huge lungfish in the lakes of mid-Cretaceous Africa where the Spinosaurs flourished.

There's so much I'll tell Fred when he's older. Funny how a thing like that, being around to tell him about dinosaurs, increases my will to live.

The Spinosaur is the largest carnivorous dinosaur there ever was. It's 55 feet long and 17,000 pounds. It has foot-long claws on six-foot arms that are strong enough to punch holes in steel. They're bipedal like T-rex and all the other theropods. They have long crocodilian jaws lined with curved, conical, interlocking teeth that are designed not to stab, cut, or crush but rather to keep hold of slippery prey and prevent them from wriggling out of its bite. It has a narrow head with nostrils high up on its slender snout so it can breathe while mostly submerged in water. It was killed by climate change 97 million years ago when North Africa cooled sharply, reducing the Spinosaur's food supply greatly.

I really do want to live long enough to tell Fred these sorts of things. Sue too, of course.

* * * * * * * * * * * *

The conference room of the newly expanded and renamed Turner Museum of the Mesozoic is a lovely space with a vaulted ceiling and graceful columns on its perimeter. Before the expansion and renovation, this whole building complex was simply called the Fossil Museum. Now it's nearly twice as large with a grand name that matches the noble aspirations of its director, our very own Clark Turner PhD. A top architectural firm from Seattle was called in to design the expansion. No expense was spared, and several further expansions are already being planned.

It's the afternoon of the same day in January 2121, and I'm sitting in the audience waiting for the opening ceremony to begin for the enlarged facility. Little Fred is with a babysitter back at the residence, and baby Sue is in the nursery there. Lana is up on the stage with Clark. He'll speak for the museum, and she'll represent Cretaceous World as a whole. I'm having her do almost all of my duties now, preparing her to be me when I'm gone.

They're married now, Lana and Clark. That happened four months ago right here in this very same space. This area wasn't open to the public yet, but it was the first part of the expansion and was ready to go by last September. Relatives came from far and wide, the inevitable awkwardness ensued, a wedding ritual was performed, everyone was festive, we all dispersed, and normal life returned. Well, anyway, normal for us.

At five minutes past the appointed hour, Lana rises and goes to the podium. The crowd becomes quiet, and she begins. She really is a charming public speaker. Far more than I am. These people here lucked out having her to watch and hear rather than me. She's basically just introducing the speaker, her husband, and so keeps her remarks fairly brief.

Clark is less enjoyable to listen to, but whatever he says is always authoritative, insightful, and filled with fervor. He's always authentic, and that gives his enthusiasm a certain charisma.

I especially like it when he reaches the part of his speech that's about the Spinosaur.

He says, "The discovery of the first fossil remains of *Spinosaurus aegyptiacus* occurred in 1912 in, of course, Egypt, as the name implies. Ernst Freiherr Stromer von Reichenbach found them and took them back with him to the Bavarian State Collection of Paleontology. These fossil fragments consisted of spines up to five feet tall and a long crocodilian-like jaw."

I find it interesting that all they had at first were the remnants of the sail on its back as well as the jawbone that indicated it was piscivorous.

Clark continues, "The fossil remains were described in words and detailed in drawings. The museum in which they were housed was unfortunately located near Nazi Party headquarters in Munich. The latter was a target for Allied bombing. When that city was bombed by the Allied Forces in April 1944, the museum was collateral damage, and the fossil pieces from *Spinosaurus aegyptiacus* were completely destroyed. Having spent 95 million years preserved in the rocks of the Saharan Desert, these fossil remnants of this amazing creature were demolished after only three decades in a museum in the center of Europe. The drawings and descriptions fortunately did survive."

I recall that the jaw was the key to figuring out this was a Tetanuran related to Baryonyx from Northern Europe, to Irritator from South America, and to Suchomimus from Sub-Saharan Africa. The sail-spines were unique to *Spinosaurus aegyptiacus* yet would lead eventually to the whole group being called spinosauroid. It was the long jaw that first indicated these four dinosaur species were close relatives.

Clark says with pride and genuine excitement, "A year ago, a nearly complete fossil of *Spinosaurus aegyptiacus* was found in Algeria. I'm delighted to say that, thanks to the generous support of Randy Winston, we now own this most important and unique treasure."

Clark pauses and holds out his arm with upward palm in the general direction of our magnanimous benefactor.

Randy nods in acknowledgement of this gesture and offers a becoming smile of modest appreciation.

The crowd applauds politely.

Clark resumes, "Our museum now has the distinction of including in its collection by far the most complete fossil of *Spinosaurus aegyptiacus* ever unearthed. This is the foundation of what will be the best spinosaurid collection in the world. Paleontologists will come from all parts of the great globe to inspect and study what is housed right here at our very own Cretaceous World."

He speaks for another hour and then turns the podium back over to Lana, who gracefully concludes the proceedings.

I think it's safe to say that Clark won't be going back to teaching at the University of Colorado or anywhere else. He's committed to us now.

Lana takes his hand and leads him over to where Randy is standing in the front row of the audience.

She says something to Randy that obviously pleases him.

Randy says something to her that she looks happy to hear.

Randy says something to Clark that gives Clark a visible surge of energy.

Clark says something rather lengthy to Randy, and Randy listens attentively.

And so on.

After a bit, Randy comes over to me.

He says, "Things seem to be going extremely well."

I smile and say, "They are. They really are."

He gives me a meaningful look and suggests, "We should have some pancakes tomorrow morning."

I know he means he wants to have a serious talk with me about developments and projections for Cretaceous World. He wants to do this at the Hominid's Delight on Main Street in neighboring Dewberry, his favorite breakfast place hereabouts.

I say, "The usual time?"

He winks, "Sounds like a plan."

* * * * * * * * * * *

Becky invented the Soup of Life when she and I became vegetarians. She wanted a basic source of protein, vitamins, minerals, and other vital nutrients that would keep me healthy through a hopefully long life. She herself preferred a huge salad with a plethora of varied ingredients that were each nutritious in its own way. I tried out calling this the Salad of Life, but it didn't stick. She just liked to call it the Big Salad.

The Soup of Life remains the foundation of my daily diet. Water, onions, celery, carrots, potatoes, quinoa, lima beans, green beans, shelled edamame, black-eyed peas, green peas, sweet corn, spinach, and brown rice: these are the ingredients that provide a sound body for my sound mind to inhabit.

Becky left me clear, concise, and detailed instructions for making the Soup of Life. Truth be told, I hate to cook. I could have the chef here at the residence do it. I don't exactly know why that doesn't appeal to me. The Soup of Life is different. I want to receive it from a woman who loves me. I don't defend this attitude of mine, and I can't really explain it. I just accept it as what is.

Lana makes me the Soup of Life now, even though she's married to Clark. She comes up from her office here at the residence and makes a week's worth in my kitchen. She divides it into seven equal portions and stores them in the refrigerator. All I have to do each day is take one of the containers out of the refrigerator, then heat and eat. Like the breast milk she stored in the refrigerator for Fred and now stores there for Sue, the Soup of Life is always on hand for me, the perennial big baby. Mama makes sure I have what I need.

I now heat my daily portion of the soup in the microwave and place the container on a tray. I also put rye bread, sliced apple, skim milk, and tea with lemon on the tray. I carefully take the tray up the spiral stairs to the tower.

There's a storm outside with driving rain and gusting wind.

I sit in the recliner chair at the center of the circular room and eat my supper.

It's the evening following the ceremony at the fossil museum.

I have a lot to think about.

I feel a bit like a sorcerer. Lana and Clark have done exactly as I wished. Lana knows it, and Clark doesn't. I'll never tell him. Lana might someday, hopefully after I'm gone. I trust her judgment.

I might as well have uttered a magical incantation:

> *A flurry, a rushing, a ringing*
> *Is passing through the glade.*
> *As if with erotic ensnaring,*
> *Life, Spirit, Mind are stayed.*

The well-qualified man and woman have united and will replace Becky and me as the couple that runs Cretaceous World in the next generation. They're also Mama and Papa to a boy and a girl for whom I am and plan to remain Grandpa. Becky will become Grandma through my stories. I'll make sure of that.

It occurs to me that I'm like the sail on a Spinosaur that isn't technically a sail.

There are all kinds of families. Becky said that more than once, and it stuck in my head. I've read a quote by Tolstoy that all happy families are the same, but that's just dogmatic nonsense. Becky's right. She's wiser than that.

I eat quietly, savoring every bite.

It seems so peaceful here in the tower, despite the storm outside.

When I've finished my meal, I put the tray on the table beside the recliner. I go over to the bookshelves and get the album I've made of Becky. I chose several hundred digital images of her and ran them through a color printer to make sheets of paper with pictures of her on them. I put these pages in a handsome binder to make an album of her persona during our time together.

Looking through the pictures of Becky in the album, I feel many emotions, most of them what you might expect: love, of course, and admiration, adoration, joy, desire, playfulness, longing.

One thing I wasn't expecting to feel is surprise that there are no children. We didn't miss them during all those decades together. We didn't want the distraction in our purposeful and peaceful life together. We were perfectly happy without children. All we needed was each other. Still, it does surprise me now.

I see the pictures from our last year alive together, and I feel the devastation and vertigo returning. We were so alone together, but we didn't feel it. All we felt was a world of love. When she was suddenly gone, the aloneness buried me alive. The weight of it was crushing, unendurable.

The gusting wind keens and moans against the windows. There's no danger. These windows are built to withstand 100 mile per hour winds. They also have steel shutters that can be deployed by remote control so they cover the windows from outside and protect them from any size wind. The rain blown against the windows runs down the glass, turning the view from the tower into blurry lights in deep darkness.

Suddenly, I have the sensation that my consciousness is all there is, that this whole scene, this unified opposition of inner and outer, is me and nothing more. I somehow feel that only I am noumenal and that all phenomena are me too.

The empty soup bowl on the table beside me strikes me as the embodiment and emblem of loneliness.

This unconventional family I'm now part of is my salvation. I couldn't bear the loneliness without it. Becky is part of it too. I insist on that.

This feels something like acceptance. It's as close as I'm likely to get anyway.

I wish I could talk with Becky about the sail of the Spinosaur. She'd understand in a way these young paleontologists just can't.

I think, "It's not clear why the sail exists. What evolutionary purpose did it serve?"

Because I'm a microbiologist addressing a biologist whom I love, I don't feel the silence.

I continue thinking, "The theory of 'the selfish gene' would have us look for a direct and immediate advantage to the survival of the individual organism as it selfishly focuses on what's good for it in the struggle against other creatures."

Becky would be perking up at this beginning.

I say out loud, "Gaia Theory and microbiology show conclusively that altruism and cooperation are also fundamental in providing an evolutionary advantage to any particular life-form. Daisyworld and the endosymbiosis of mitochondria and chloroplasts establish this beyond all reasonable doubt."

Becky would now enter into the conversation, and a long and most satisfying discussion would ensue.

The rain keeps landing sideways on the window panes like little splashes of darkness and light.

OTHER
ANAPHORA LITERARY
PRESS TITLES

PLJ: Interviews with Gene Ambaum and Corban Addison: VII:3, Fall 2015
Editor: Anna Faktorovich

Architecture of Being
By: Bruce Colbert

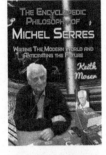

The Encyclopedic Philosophy of Michel Serres
By: Keith Moser

Forever Gentleman
By: Roland Colton

Janet Yellen
By: Marie Bussing-Burks

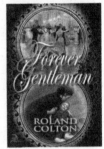

Diseases, Disorders, and Diagnoses of Historical Individuals
By: William J. Maloney

Armageddon at Maidan
By: Vasyl Baziv

Vovochka
By: Alexander J. Motyl

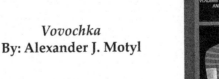

CPSIA information can be obtained
at www.ICGtesting.com
Printed in the USA
BVOW04*0444200417

481166BV00003B/3/P